"Anna Taborska's fiction combir
cruelty and evil with a deep cc
from it. Stark imagery and psychological truth are the hallmarks
of her work; she's a powerful writer we'll be hearing a lot more
from in years to come."

Simon Bestwick, author of *Tide of Souls* and *The Faceless*

"… surely among the grimmest contemporary horror authors
(I mean that as a compliment) …"

Demonik, Vault of Evil

"Anna Taborska's fantastic, surreal, dark fantasy … is still
seared in my memory."

Colin Leslie, The Heart of Horror

"… nothing short of chilling."

Tom Johnstone, The Zone

For Those Who Dream Monsters

Anna Taborska

Mortbury Press

Published by Mortbury Press

First Edition

2013

All stories in this collection copyright © Anna Taborska

Illustrations and introduction copyright © Reggie Oliver

Cover art copyright © Steve Upham

ISBN 978-1-910030-01-1

Mortbury Press
Shiloh
Nant-Glas
Llandrindod Wells
Powys
LD1 6PD

mortburypress@yahoo.com
http://mortburypress.webs.com/

For those who dream monsters.

INTRODUCTION

It is not supposed to be a good thing to be in someone's black books. An exception may be made in the case of Charles Black's ground-breaking Black Books of Horror. I have read many excellent stories in his anthologies and have met their authors and found them to be, without exception, very delightful people. Since joining Charles's 'stable' I can proudly number among my friends not only Charles himself but many of his writers, including John Llewellyn Probert, Thana Niveau, Kate Farrell, Mark Samuels, Simon K. Unsworth, and Anna Taborska.

I first encountered Anna Taborska's work in the sixth of Charles's Black Books. The story was called 'Bagpuss' – it is included in this volume – and I was immediately struck by its originality and the excellence of its writing. Here is an authentic and exciting new voice in horror writing, I thought. I immediately got hold of and read whatever stories by her that I could, and my subsequent readings more than confirmed the first impression.

The truth is that in all genres, and perhaps that of 'horror' in particular, writers tend to fall into certain easily recognisable styles and themes. They move along predetermined grooves, and they may do so well or badly, but in so doing they produce work which is not distinguishable from the general run, and therefore, in the end, not very distinguished. Anna's work has an individual feel about it, a personality. She has a very acute sense of personal suffering which is conveyed in poignant but never excessive detail. She does not commit the fault to which most minor writers of horror are prone, that of making her 'victims' mere cyphers, puppets into whom the storyteller can stick pins at will and without conscience. There is real pain in these stories and the horror is conveyed on a deep psychological level.

Nor is she one of those writers who, in their individuality, pursue one particular theme or atmosphere to destruction. "Damn him, he is so various!" said Gainsborough in exasperation at his contemporary and rival Sir Joshua Reynolds, and the same could be said of Anna Taborska. Here in one generous volume are eighteen stories in a variety of settings: the United Kingdom, the United States, Africa, Eastern Europe, the present, the past. She deals movingly with the matter of the Nazi Occupation of Poland and the Holocaust ('Arthur's Cellar', 'The Girl in the Blue Coat') but from a very personal and individual angle. 'Dirty Dybbuk' is a story based on Jewish folk myth; others such as 'Rusalka' and 'First Night' take their inspiration from Europe's rich tradition of fairy tale and legend. We enter the film world for 'Cut!' and that of non-governmental organisations for 'Buy a Goat for Christmas'. There is mordant satire in 'Tea with the Devil' and an exploration of our deepest and darkest fears in 'Underbelly'. There are wolves in 'Little Pig'; there is witchery – or imagined witchery – in 'The Creaking'. I could go on, but I would become exhausted: readers should have the pleasure of discovering for themselves how constantly Anna Taborska breaks new ground. "Damn her, she is so various!"

And yet, and yet... Through all this wonderful diversity runs the thread of a particular sensibility: a very deep compassion for the sufferings of humanity, and a poetic quality in the writing that suddenly lifts horror into a world of strange and terrible beauty. Anna is the daughter of a great Polish poet, and a poet herself: it shows.

It is for these reasons that I asked Anna if I might do some illustrations for her first volume of stories. I have hitherto only illustrated my own work and have no plans to do so for anyone else, but Anna Taborska's work has a special quality which evokes powerful and seductive visual imagery. This is hardly surprising since Anna is an award winning film maker, a mistress of the moving image. It is something we have in common: we both have a background in the performing arts, albeit slightly different branches. I began my career as an actor and playwright, and I tend to write my stories in 'scenes' as a result; Anna, from her more film-orientated perspective, does the same, and this is what gives her work its dynamic quality as well as its strong visual stimulus.

Introduction

I immensely enjoyed entering the strange and terrible world of Taborska. Many of the stories prompted not one but several vivid images, but I decided that one per story was quite enough: any more might prove too tiring both for me and the reader. I can truthfully say that any merit these illustrations have can be directly attributable to Anna's pen rather than mine.

Of one other thing I can assure the reader: there is more to come from that pen of Anna's and it will be of the same devastatingly high quality.

Reggie Oliver
Suffolk, August 2013

SCHRÖDINGER'S HUMAN

The cat had the uncanny ability of seeming to be in two places at once, and it appeared logical to the man that he should name it Schrödinger. The cat evidently approved of the name, purring as the man tried it out.

"Well, Schrödinger, I expect you *must* want some dinner *today*?" the man asked, backing away from the plate of cat food to allow the animal a chance to feed. But the cat stayed where it was, high up on the kitchen cupboard, and refused to give the cat food the time of day, just as it had refused milk and water, and even ham.

The man had first come across the cat on his return from work the previous day. It was thin and dirty, a mud-smeared black, with cold green eyes and a tattered left ear. The pitiful-looking thing was stretched out on his doorstep and refused to budge, even as the man approached. Instead, it fixed him with an expectant stare and weaved its tail from side to side. The man studied the cat, and a long-forgotten joy stirred within him.

Ever since he was a child, the man had enjoyed torturing animals. His grandfather had bought him a butterfly net, and the boy quickly worked out that if you rubbed too much of the colourful dust off a butterfly's wings, it had trouble flying. And things got even more interesting if you pulled off its wings altogether and put it on an anthill. You could watch the black specks of the ants swarm all over the wounded intruder; watch the butterfly that was no longer a butterfly, but a fascinating broken thing, try to lift itself out of the writhing mass of small stinging creatures, helplessly flailing its long thin legs, its proboscis furling and unfurling in some strange insect rhythm of pain.

Butterflies continued to fascinate for a long time, but eventually the allure of real animals – one which screamed and bled – took over from those that merely twitched pathetically. After much begging and family debate, he was finally given an air rifle for his birthday, but sadly this was confiscated when he moved up from shooting crows and squirrels to shooting the neighbours' pets.

If necessity is the mother of invention, then a twisted imagination is its father, aunt and uncle. The boy came to understand that the air rifle, which he had so mourned, wasn't even a drop in the endless ocean of possibilities when it came to inflicting suffering on anything small and fluffy that had a heartbeat. And the smaller and fluffier it was, the easier it could be lured with a warm tone of voice, a friendly smile, a tickle behind the ear and, if all else failed, a piece of ham.

The boy tried a variety of techniques on his victims: dismemberment, disembowelment, decapitation, throwing off the roof or out of a window, the breaking of individual bones with a blunt instrument, bloodletting, crucifixion, and even electrocution – he was particularly good at this, as he had an excellent science teacher at school and displayed a definite propensity for the subject. But his favourite was luring a cat with the promise of food or affection, locking it in a cage and carrying it to his parents' roof, where he would douse its tail with petrol and set it alight before pushing it headfirst down the drainpipe. The trapped animal, its tail ablaze, would scream all the way down the drainpipe until it got stuck in a bend, where it would burn to charred bones and then fall out the bottom. This method only worked on small cats and kittens, but could also be extended to some breeds of puppy. The boy's attempts to involve the little girl next door in his pastime resulted in his being sent to a boarding school run by monks, where his sadistic horizons expanded to the use of canes, whips and rulers.

The boy left school with top results in science and went on to university, where his interest in animals waned somewhat, as his physics studies and unreciprocated fascination with girls led him to attain a First Class degree, despite almost being sent down for peeping through a female student's bedroom window. He stayed on in academia, eventually becoming a lecturer at a reputable university, where he could continue to indulge in physics and his unreciprocated fascination with girls.

And now here he was, trying to get home after a tiring day of lectures, and this scruffy, ugly cat was lying on his doorstep, as if daring him to gouge out its eyes and cut off its paws. Old passions awoke within the man, but he was too tired to act on them. He picked up a piece of brick that was lying in the roadside and aimed it between the cat's eyes. Just then a piercing pain shot through the man's temple. He dropped the brick and put his hands up to his head. As quickly as it had come, the pain was gone, but the man was left feeling bewildered and a little dizzy. As he rubbed his eyes to clear his head, he heard a voice close by his ear.

"Let me in," it said.

The man spun round, but there was nobody nearby – only the cat sprawled on his doorstep, eyeing him like a scientist eyes a mildly interesting specimen before dissection.

"Let me in," the voice continued, "and I'll show you things you've never seen ... I'll take you to places you can't begin to imagine."

The man closed his eyes for a moment. When he opened them, the voice was gone and he felt his normal self again. He looked at his front door; the cat was no longer reclining, but sat alertly a couple of feet away from the door, as if waiting for the man to open it.

What the hell? thought the man. If the cat wanted to come in, then let it. He was tired now, but he would amuse himself with the animal later. He opened the door and stood back to let the cat in. It eyed him suspiciously for a moment, then darted past, leaping over the threshold and heading straight for the kitchen.

The man followed it, locking the door behind him. He put his briefcase down in the hallway and went to see what the cat was doing. The kitchen was bathed in darkness and before the man switched on the light, he caught sight of the cat's eyes glowing in the shadows by the sink. But as the light from the overhead lamp illuminated the room, the man saw that the cat was not by the sink. Surprised, he looked around and spotted the creature sitting high on a kitchen cupboard, peering down at him with some curiosity and possibly a hint of malevolence.

"Well I'll be damned," he told the cat. "The rough and tumble world of quantum physics would have a field day with you." The man laughed at his own wit and went to the fridge to get some milk. If he was to get any use out of the cat, he'd have to start by getting it down from the kitchen cupboard.

But no end of coaxing would bring the cat down from its vantage point – not even a slice of premium ham. The man contemplated standing on a chair and dislodging the cat or throwing something at it, but he really couldn't be bothered. Besides, it would be much more fun to get the cat to trust him and then see the surprise in its furry little face when he took his penknife to it. The man made his own dinner, ate it and went through to the sitting room to mark first-year physics assignments, leaving a plate of ham out to see if the cat would come down in his absence.

That night the man dreamt that he was walking through an unfamiliar landscape of red and black. The landscape was constantly shifting and changing. One moment he was walking along a mountain path, looking down into a valley of houses and fields, next he was in a labyrinth of tunnels, the walls made of human bones and skulls arranged in intricate patterns, one on top of the other. Somewhere ahead of the man a fire burned, and light from it bounced around the bone walls, bathing them in a warm glow and sending shadows flitting around the man. Beside him walked Schrödinger the cat, watching him with a modicum of curiosity, as if all this was familiar to the animal and it was merely interested in what the man made of it all – interested, but not *that* interested.

As the man approached the source of the flames, he became aware of the crackling sound they made. The crackling became a scratching, and the scratching grew louder until the man awoke. The scratching continued and the man realised that it was coming from his wardrobe. The damned cat had somehow got into it and was probably ruining his suits. He reached over to switch on his bedside lamp and recoiled as his fingers touched fur. The man sat upright and the cat leapt off the bedside table on which it had been sitting.

"Goddamn you, Schrödinger!" The man switched on the lamp and glared at the creature now sitting in the doorway. He swung his legs out of bed, but the cat had already gone. The man closed his bedroom door and went back to sleep.

In the morning the cat was back on the kitchen cupboard, and the ham was untouched on the plate where the man had left it the night before. The creature obviously hadn't eaten for a while and it had to be hungry. Either it was sick or it had been trained not to eat anything other than cat food. The man determined to buy some *Whiskas* on his way home from work.

But the cat wouldn't eat *Whiskas*, or *Meow Mix* or *Friskies*. It wouldn't drink milk or water and it wouldn't eat cat biscuits. In fact, it was a miracle that it was still alive. It was growing more emaciated by the day, and its protruding ribs only served to make it look scruffier and uglier. For a moment the man astonished himself by contemplating taking it to a vet, but quickly shrugged off such an insane idea and decided to kill it. He placed a kitchen chair next to the cupboard on which Schrödinger was perched, and went to get the meat cleaver. Then the doorbell rang.

The man put down the cleaver and went to answer the door. It was the teenage girl from the house next door.

"I'm sorry to bother you," she said, "but I'm locked out of the house. I forgot to take my keys this morning and my mum isn't back till seven. A couple of workmen followed me home from the high street and I don't want to wait outside. Can I hang out at yours until my mum gets back?"

The man studied the girl's short skirt and the way her blonde hair was pulled back in a ponytail, revealing the curve where her neck met her shoulder.

"Sure," he told the girl and stood aside to let her in. He cast a quick glance around the street. Sure enough, he saw two workmen loitering across the road, but they quickly turned on their heels and disappeared. There was no one else around.

"Would you like a cup of tea?" the man asked, leading the way to the kitchen.

"No thanks. Have you got any coke?"

"Yes." The man got a coke from the fridge and handed it to the girl. "Would you like a glass?"

"No thanks." The man indicated for the girl to take a seat. That was when they both saw Schrödinger. It was standing on the kitchen table, tail twitching, staring at the girl.

"Oh, what a cute kitty!" cried the girl and moved towards the animal.

"Schrödinger, what the hell are you doing?" The tone in the man's voice stopped the girl in her tracks. The man moved forward, ready to swipe the cat off the table, but as he did so, the sharp pain in his head came, then went, and a voice near his ear said, "Kill her!"

"What?" exclaimed the man.

"What?" asked the girl, staring at the man uncomprehendingly.

"Nothing, honey, nothing."

But the voice came again, more persistent this time: "Kill her … now!"

The man felt confused. He looked at the girl. Her tanned arms and legs looked so inviting. A small artery in her neck was throbbing. The man found himself wondering how far the blood from that artery would spurt and whether it would reach the ceiling or just spatter the walls. He wondered whether the look of surprise in her eyes would be like that of the kittens and puppies he had dispatched to kitten and puppy heaven as a boy. He suspected that it would be better – much better – than anything he had experienced before. His cock was throbbing and he realised that the cat was staring at him, green eyes blazing, its customary disdain replaced by a feral excitement.

The artery in the girl's neck was still throbbing. Her lips were cherry red and a look of alarm was creeping over her face. She raised her hand to cover her mouth and, as she did so, her top rode up a little and the man could see the silver ring in her pierced belly button. As time seemed to stop then stretch around the man, he noticed that the blue of the small gemstone on the ring matched the colour of the girl's eyes.

The artery in the girl's neck was throbbing, the man's cock was throbbing, and now a blood vessel in his head started to throb. The light in the kitchen seemed to throb and then the whole world was throbbing – a glorious red throbbing, pulsating, pounding. Then the meat cleaver was in the man's hand and the look of surprise in the girl's eyes was better than the puppies and the kittens – it was better than anything the man had experienced before, and the girl's blood was on the walls and on the ceiling and on the floor.

When the throbbing subsided, the man was sitting on the floor, his hands and clothes covered in blood. He felt calm and he felt good. The cat was standing beside him, face and whiskers stained red, frenziedly lapping up the girl's blood from the floor. The man stared at the animal in disbelief, but made no move to stop it. Despite the blood on its snout, the cat seemed less dirty than before: its fur seemed sleeker, it seemed somehow fatter and healthier, even its tattered ear seemed to have grown back together.

"Goddamn you, Schrödinger," the man said quietly, but the cat didn't even acknowledge his presence. It had licked the vast amount of blood off the floor and was now licking the girl's fingers. The man crawled around the girl's body to the hand that wasn't being worked on by the cat. He lifted the hand and sucked the blood from the index finger. It had a sickly taste, sweet and metallic. The man sucked on the girl's thumb and found that the taste was no longer sickly; it was, in fact, rather good.

A feeling of contented tiredness overcame the man, and he dozed off right there, on the kitchen floor, next to the girl's lacerated body. When he woke up it was dark and Schrödinger was nowhere to be seen. The man chopped up the girl's body with the meat cleaver, removing clothes, hair, bones and anything else that was inedible – this he would take to the municipal dump on his way to work tomorrow, along with the girl's faceless head. Everything else he washed and divided between his fridge and the freezer. He cleaned the walls as best he could, then dragged the kitchen table across and attempted to clean the ceiling. He would have to buy a large tin of emulsion and paint over the stains that wouldn't wash off.

That night the man dreamt that he was standing over a precipice, looking down into a vast pit. The pit was filled with fire. The man noticed movement in the flames and realised that the pit was full of people – thousands of people – burning. He found that if he concentrated, he could hone in on individuals. He could clearly see the expressions of torment on their faces, the pain in their eyes. Their bodies were writhing and their limbs flailing about helplessly. The man remembered the wingless butterflies flailing around on the anthill in his parents' garden, and smiled.

He looked down and saw Schrödinger gazing up at him, reflections of the flames dancing in the animal's eyes.

Next morning the man awoke to purring by the side of his bed, but wasn't all that surprised to find that Schrödinger was not by his bed at all, but was waiting expectantly in the kitchen, sitting by the spot where the man had previously left its unwanted plate of cat food.

"Oh, so now you want to eat?"

The man knew what the cat wanted, but decided to tease it and put out a bowl of milk. But the joke was on him, as Schrödinger gave him such a look of malevolent contempt that the man's blood seemed to freeze in his veins and a nasty shiver went down his spine.

"Sorry," he said, and poured the milk down the sink. He got out a mincing machine and took some of the girl's flesh out of the fridge. He pushed it into the mincer and watched the pink worms come out the bottom. A sharp meow distracted him, and he glanced down to see Schrödinger dancing around on its hind paws, teeth bared. He put the mince on a clean plate, and hardly had time to place the plate on the floor before Schrödinger was upon it, wolfing down the meat as if it hadn't eaten in days. The man couldn't help thinking that if he hadn't withdrawn his hand in time, the animal might have devoured that too.

As he watched the cat feed, the man noticed how healthy it was looking. He thought he might have imagined it last night – in all the excitement, but in the cold light of day he could see that the cat's fur was a sleek, clean, shiny black, its protruding ribs had disappeared – concealed by a respectable plumpness – and its left ear looked like it had never encountered the Mike Tyson of the feline world.

The man cut a few thin slices of meat, and treated himself to a full English breakfast.

Over the next couple of weeks the cat and the man ate what was left of the teenager. The police came round and asked questions, but only the two workmen had seen the girl enter the man's house, and the police knew nothing of their existence. Officer Jones commented on the man's cute cat and Schrödinger purred obligingly, and that was that. Or would have been, except that the man couldn't stop thinking about the girl. Sometimes he worried about getting found out, but mostly he reminisced about the unbearably sweet sensation of plunging the meat cleaver into her soft flesh. His craving for more flesh and more blood wouldn't let him rest or concentrate on his work. Despite their shared diet, as the cat got fatter and silkier, the man lost weight, grew pale and haggard. When he slept, he dreamt of the burning pit and the bodies in it, writhing in perpetual torment. But mostly he just tossed and turned in bed, listened to Schrödinger scratching in the wardrobe and watched its eyes glow by the side of his bed.

About the time that the girl meat ran out, the man's cravings reached an unbearable pitch. He was horny and hungry and confused all at the same time. He was distracted in his tutorials and it was just a matter of time before one of the students complained. Schrödinger was refusing to eat anything that wasn't human, and its body was atrophying. Its left ear was hanging in tatters by the side of its head, and its teeth started falling out, so that its tongue protruded, giving it a rather unsavoury and slightly demented expression. It eyed the man with barely disguised contempt, and the man found himself feeling increasingly uncomfortable around it.

The student was only in her first term, but she was already behind in her work. She had been good at physics at school, but university was different. The professor was bombarding them with new information every day, and they were expected to come up with their own ideas and solutions to problems. When the professor asked to see her, she was terrified that she was in trouble. She was relieved when he spoke kindly to her and offered to spend some time with her, going over problems they had tackled in class, to help her catch up with the others. The professor explained that he had a variety of textbooks at home and it would be easier if she dropped by his house, where they would have all the books at hand.

"I realise that young ladies sometimes feel uncomfortable being alone with a man," he told her, "and you are very welcome to bring a friend with you, as long as your friend won't mind keeping my cat company while we're studying."

"You have a cat?" the girl smiled.

"His name's Schrödinger. He's very friendly and he's especially fond of young ladies."

The girl smiled again and lowered her eyes.

"Do you have a friend you would like to bring?"

The man knew full well that the girl had no friends. Shy and from a state school, unlike the privileged majority of the students, he often saw her sitting alone in the lecture hall and leaving alone when the lectures were over.

"Oh, that's okay," the girl replied. "I don't feel uncomfortable."

"Well, that's just fine. My cat would love to meet you. He's been feeling a little under the weather lately."

The plan seemed fool proof, but when the student arrived at his house, the man found himself having second thoughts. This was not something he'd envisaged – he'd wanted another girl desperately for weeks. But when he saw her standing on his doorstep in her knee high socks and pink sweater, physics notes in a file under her arm, his palms suddenly felt clammy and a nerve under his eye started to twitch. She was his student, after all, and maybe that meant that he was crossing some kind of line – a line between fair game and ... well ... not.

"Come in," he told the girl, seriously considering actually giving her a physics lesson. But as soon as he shut the door behind her and ushered her into the kitchen, Schrödinger was there in front of them, meowing and twitching its tail.

"Oh," exclaimed the girl, "he doesn't look too well."

"He hasn't been eating properly," the man explained. "In fact, he's been feeling rather sorry for himself, but I'm sure he'll cheer up now that you're here."

The girl stooped down to stroke the cat, but something in its unappetising appearance and intent stare put her off. She straightened up and smiled at the professor, who offered her a cup of tea and put the kettle on.

The cat meowed loudly and the man tried to swipe at it behind the girl's back. But the pain in his head was back. The man winced and clapped his hands to his temples.

"Are you okay, professor?" There was concern in the girl's brown eyes.

But the pain in his head was gone, the dizzy feeling was back, and the voice was telling him to kill.

"Professor? Are you feeling alright?"

But the kettle was in his hand and, before he knew it, he was pouring boiling water over the girl's face and she was too shocked to make a sound as her face started to blister. And then he was bashing the girl over the head with the kettle, bashing her face and bashing her chest and bashing the base of her skull. The girl slid to the floor, but still he kept hitting her. He could feel his skin burning as some of the boiling liquid splashed on his hands, but still he kept smashing the girl with the kettle until her head was a bloody pulp and her legs ceased twitching. Then he stopped. He put the kettle down and went to the sink, soaking his hands under the cold water tap until he was fairly confident that they wouldn't blister. He glanced occasionally over his shoulder at the cat, which was greedily lapping up the puddle of blood beneath the dead girl's head.

The cleaning and carving took a long time and the man went to bed exhausted. He fell asleep quickly and dreamt that he was falling into the burning pit. He fell slowly, and had ample opportunity to watch and feel the flames getting closer. The rising heat overtook him on his way down and, by the time he reached the bottom of the pit, his flesh was already blistering and smoking. His skin caught fire and was burnt away, and, as the flames reached the fat beneath, the man went up like a torch. He tried to scream, but his throat was burning on the inside. He looked up and saw Schrödinger looking down at him from the edge of the pit. The cat's expression was one of mild amusement.

The following day the man determined to kill Schrödinger. He minced some meat, laid it out on a clean plate and put it down in front of the waiting cat. While the creature was preoccupied, the man opened the drawer and took hold of the meat cleaver. The pain hit his head like a spear and he dropped the cleaver back in the drawer. He looked over at Schrödinger, but the cat didn't even interrupt its meal long enough to cast him an evil glance.

It was a while before anyone reported the student missing. The police came to the campus and interviewed everyone who knew her. The interviews didn't last long, as even those students who recognised her picture weren't able to provide any information about the girl. But Officer Jones recognised the physics professor as the next-door neighbour he had interviewed in his previous unsolved missing girl case, and decided to pay him a home visit, complete with warrant.

Officer Jones arrived at the house with two other policemen. If the man was shocked to see three police officers on his doorstep, he didn't show it. He invited them in politely and stood back as they ransacked his home.

Officer Jones spotted a pair of green eyes in the shadows under the coffee table in the sitting room, and remembered the man's cat. He had a soft spot for cats and bent down to the animal, but saw to his surprise that the space under the coffee table was empty. As he straightened up, he noticed the cat sitting on an armchair at the far side of the room, watching him. Before he had a chance to approach the animal, one of the other officers summoned him from the bedroom. He hurried over to his colleague.

Officer Trevayne was standing by the open drawer of the man's bedside cabinet, holding a silver belly button ring with a small blue gemstone in his latex-gloved hand. Jones recognised it immediately from a photograph given to him by the parents of the missing girl from the house next door. He moved rapidly out into the hallway, where Officer Green was waiting with the man.

"Sir, we need you to come with us to the station, to answer some questions," Jones told the man. For the briefest moment the man looked shaken, but regained his composure almost instantly.

"Of course," he said. "Anything I can do to help... I'll just grab my coat." The man went over to the coat stand and reached for his coat, but just then he felt the familiar stabbing pain in his head. It came and went, leaving him confused as to how it was that he'd lifted the heavy coat stand and why it was that he brought the full weight of it down on Officer Green – brought the large wooden object down again and again on the policeman, until he felt a stinging pain rip through his shoulder, and the whole world went red, then black.

Jones put his gun away and radioed for an ambulance. He moved swiftly over to the man and checked his pulse; the bullet had passed straight through his heart and the man was dead within seconds. It was a bad situation, but the man would have killed Officer Green – if he hadn't already done so. Jones knelt beside Officer Trevayne, who was tending to their badly wounded colleague.

"He's alive," said Trevayne, "but he needs to get to a hospital ASAP."

"I'll go outside and flag down the ambulance."

But as Jones moved towards the front door, he felt a sharp pain in his temple. He winced and put his hand up to his head, but the pain was gone, replaced by a slight feeling of nausea and bewilderment. This in turned passed, and a voice spoke in the policeman's ear.

"Take me with you," it said. "I'll show you things you've never seen."

Officer Jones looked round and saw the black cat eyeing him dispassionately.

LITTLE PIG

Adam waited nervously in the International Arrivals hall of
Heathrow Airport's Terminal 1. Born and bred in London, Adam
had never thought of himself as the type of guy who would
import a wife from Poland. His parents had made sure that he'd
learnt Polish from an early age; while his English friends had
played football or watched *Swap Shop* on Saturday mornings,
Adam had been dragged kicking and screaming to Polish classes
in Ealing. But it had all paid off in the end when he went to
Poland one summer and met Krystyna. Since that time, the
smart, pretty brunette had relocated to London and moved in
with Adam. They were engaged to be married, and it seemed to

Adam that all the members of his fiancé's family had already
visited London and stayed with them – all, that is, except
Krystyna's grandmother, and that was who Adam was now
waiting for. Krystyna had not been able to get the day off work,
and Adam was now anxiously eyeing every elderly woman who
came through the arrival gate, in the hope that one of them would
match the tattered photograph that Krystyna had given him.

Eventually a little old lady came out alone. Adam recognised
her immediately and started to walk towards her, stopping
abruptly as he saw the woman slip, drop her glasses and, in a
desperate effort to right herself, step on them, crushing them
completely. Upset for the woman, Adam began to rush forward,
only to halt as she started to laugh hysterically. She muttered
something under her breath and, had he not known any better,
Adam could have sworn that what she said was "little pig!"

The sleigh sped through the dark forest, the scant moonlight
reflected by the snow lighting up the whites of the horse's eyes
as it galloped along the narrow path, nostrils flaring and velvet
mouth spitting foam and blood into the night. The woman cried
out as the reins cut into her hands, and screamed to her children
to hang on.

The three little girls clung to each other and to the sides of the
sleigh, their tears freezing onto their faces as soon as they
formed. The corner of the large blanket in which their mother
had wrapped them for the perilous journey to their grandparents'
house had come loose and was flapping violently in the icy air.

"Hold on to Vitek!" the woman screamed over her shoulder at
her eldest child, her voice barely audible over the howling wind.
But the girl did not need to be told; only two days away from her
seventh birthday, she clung onto her baby brother, fear for her
tiny sibling stronger than her own terror. The other two girls,
aged two and four, huddled together, lost in an incomprehensible
world of snow and fear and darkness.

The woman whipped the reins against the horse's heaving
flanks, but the animal was already running on a primal fear
stronger than pain. The excited yelps audible over the snowstorm

left little doubt in the woman's mind: the pack was gaining on the sleigh – the hungry wolves were getting closer.

That winter had been particularly hard on the wolf pack. The invading Russian army had taken the peasants' livestock and, with no farm animals to snatch, the wolves had been limited to seeking out those rabbits and wild fowl that the desperate peasants and fleeing refugees had not killed and eaten. Driven half-mad with starvation, the wolves had already invested an irrevocable amount of energy in chasing the horse, and instinct informed them that it was too late to give up now – they had to feed or had to die.

The horse was wheezing, the blood freezing in its nostrils as it strained through the snow. Its chestnut coat was matted with sweat whipped up into a dirty foam. Steam rose off its back like smoke, giving the bizarre impression that the animal was on fire.

The woman shouted at the horse, willing it on, and brought the reins down against its flanks. She had only been fending for herself for three days – since the soldiers had tied her husband to a tree, cut off his genitals and sawn him in half with a blunt saw – but she knew instinctively that without the horse she and her children would die. If the starving wolves did not kill them, the cold would. They still had many miles to travel – and they would never make it on foot. The time had come to resort to the last hope her children had left.

The woman pulled on the reins, slowing the horse to a more controlled pace. She tied the reins to the sleigh, the horse running steadily along the forest path. She tried not to look at her shaking, crying children, clinging onto each other as they were thrown around the sleigh – the pitiful sight would break her, and she must not break. She must not lose the battle to keep her children alive.

"Good girls," she muttered, without looking back, "hold on to your brother." She stood up carefully in the speeding sleigh and reached over the side, unfastening the buckles on the wicker basket attached there. She opened the lid as slowly and as carefully as the shaking sleigh would allow. The sight that greeted her made her stomach turn, as fear for her children gave way to shock and panic. She howled in despair. A sudden jerky movement sent her sprawling back into the sleigh. She pulled herself up and clawed at the basket again, tearing the whole thing off in an effort to change the unchangeable.

"Little pig!" screamed the woman, her eyes wild and unseeing. The children screamed too, the madness in their mother's voice destroying the last remnant of safety and order in their world. "Little pig!" she screamed. "They took the little pig!"

The woman fell back onto her seat. The horse was slowing. An expectant howl pierced the darkness behind the sleigh. The woman grabbed the reins and struck at the horse's flanks again. The animal snorted and strained onwards, but even in her panic the woman knew that if she tried to force any more speed out of it, she would kill it, and all her children with it.

The howling and snarling grew closer, forcing the horse's fear onto a new level. It reared and tried to bolt, almost overturning the sleigh, but its exhaustion and the snow prevented its escape from the hungry pack.

The wolves were beginning to fan out on either side of the sleigh, still behind it, but not far off. One of the beasts – a battle-scarred individual with protruding ribs and cold yellow eyes – broke away from the others and made a dash for the horse, nipping at its heels. The horse screamed and kicked out, catching the wolf across the snout and sending it tumbling into the trees. It pulled itself up in seconds and started back after its companions.

The reins almost slipped from the woman's bleeding, freezing hands. She tightened her grip, wrapping the reins around her wrists. If only they were closer to her parents' village, she could let the wolves have the horse – it was the horse that they were after. But without the horse they would all freeze in the snow long before they reached safety.

The pack was catching up with the sleigh now; the wolves spilled forward, biting at the horse. The woman shouted at the wolves, whipped at them and at the horse with the reins, but there was nothing she could do. She cast a glance at her daughters: the two little ones pale as sheets, Irena holding onto Vitek as if he were life itself. And Vitek – her perfect little boy.

The woman remembered her husband's face when she first told him he had a son. His face had lit up; he had taken the little boy from her and held him in his big, strong arms ... her husband ... then an image of the last time she had seen him – seen his mutilated corpse tied to the old walnut tree in the orchard...

She was back in the present, fighting to save her children – losing the fight to save her children. The little pig was gone – she had put it in the wicker basket at the side of the sleigh and fastened the straps when the soldiers were getting drunk inside her house. She had gone back to the barn to get the children, to flee with them under cover of darkness to what she hoped would be the relative safety of her parents' village. Someone must have seen her put the little pig in the basket, someone cruel enough to take the time to do up the straps after sentencing her children to death in the wolf-infested forest.

The little pig was gone and another sacrifice was needed in its place to protect the horse. The woman prepared to jump out of the sleigh. She turned to Irena and shouted, "Give Vitek to Kasia!" Irena stared at her mother blankly. "Give your brother to Kasia!" The woman's voice rose to a hysterical pitch. Four-year-old Kasia clung onto her two-year-old sister, and Irena began to cry, clutching her brother even tighter. "Give him to her!" screamed the woman, "I need you to hold the reins!" But even as she said it, she knew that the six-year-old would never be able to control the terrified horse. Her own hands were a bloody ruin and she wondered how she was able to hang on as the frantic animal fought its way forward.

"Irena! Give Vitek to Kasia – now!" But Irena saw something in her mother's eyes that scared her more than the dark and the shaking sleigh and even the wolves. She clutched her brother to her chest and shook her head, fresh tears rolling down her face and freezing to her cheeks.

A large silver wolf clamped its jaws onto the horse's left hind leg. The horse stumbled, but managed to right itself and the wolf let go, unable to keep up with the horse in the deep snow – but not for long. As the chestnut reeled, the sleigh lurched and the woman panicked. She had to act now or lose all her children. She could not give her life for them because they would never make it to safety without her. But a sacrifice had to be made. If she could not die to save her children, then one of them would have to die to save the others. She would not lose them all. One of them would have to die and she would have to choose. The delicate fabric of the woman's sanity was finally stretched to its limits and gave way. She threw back her head and howled her anguish into the night. All around her the night howled back.

The woman turned and looked into the faces of her children. A sharp intake of breath – like that taken by one about to drown. She took the reins in one hand, and with the other she reached out for her beloved son – her husband's greatest joy; the frailest of her children, half-frozen despite his sister's efforts to keep him warm, too exhausted even to cry, and the least likely to survive the journey.

"Give him to me!" she screamed at Irena. The girl struggled with her mother. The woman wrenched her baby out of her daughter's grasp and held him to her, gazing for a moment into his eyes. The woman smiled through her tears at her son. Snow was falling on the baby's upturned face, the frost had tinged his lips a pale blue, but in the woman's fevered mind, her baby smiled back at her.

Two of the wolves had closed in on the horse and were trying to bring it down. The woman screamed and threw Vitek as far from the sleigh as she could. There was a moment's silence, then a triumphant yelping as the wolves turned their attention away from the horse, and rushed away into the night. Irena cried out, and her little sisters stared uncomprehendingly at their mother, who screamed and screamed as she grabbed the reins in both hands and whipped the horse on into the dark.

As the first light of dawn broke across the horizon, an eerie sight greeted the sleepy village. The sleigh rolled in slowly, as the exhausted horse made it within sight of the first farmhouse. It stood for a moment, head drooping, blood seeping from its nostrils, its mouth, from open wounds along its flanks. Then it dropped silently to the ground and lay still.

Little Pig

In the sleigh sat a wild-eyed woman, staring but unseeing, her black hair streaked with white, reins clenched tightly in her bloody hands. Behind her were three little girls. Two were slumped together, asleep. The third girl, the eldest of the three, was awake – she sat very still, eyes wide, silent as her mother.

"Irena?" Adam reached the old lady and touched her arm. "I'm Adam." He bent down and picked up what was left of Irena's glasses. "I'm sorry about your glasses," he told her, handing the crushed frames back to her.

"No need to be sorry," said Irena. "It's just a little pig."

Adam was taken aback. It was bad enough taking care of Krystyna's relatives, but she had never said that her grandmother was senile.

Irena read Adam like an open book.

"A little pig," she explained, "a small sacrifice to make sure nothing really terrible happens ... during my visit."

"I understand," said Adam. He did not understand, but at least there was some method in the old lady's madness, and that was good enough for him. He paid the parking fee at the ticket machine, and they left the building: a tall young man pushing a trolley and a little old lady clutching a pair of broken glasses.

FISH

Have you ever come face to face with a frightened scorpion fish? Harry Tomlinson has. A row of venomous barbs and a pair of startled fishy eyes only centimetres from his own, and coming closer. A flurry of bubbles as Harry's breath escaped him, then he was hurtling backwards and upwards as his head was yanked out of the tank once more.

"Where is it?" shouted the brick shithouse of a man who had Harry by the hair, and whose name seemed to be Tiny. Harry choked for breath, coughing up fish-tank water and miniature pebbles. Tiny held Harry, while his buddy – a man whose name

Harry had ascertained to be Frank – punched the retching postman in the stomach.

"I don't know what you're talking about," gasped Harry. "I told you, you've got the wrong man." Frank signalled to Tiny to carry on. "No!" protested Harry, fear for his beloved prickly pet stronger than fear for his own life. He struggled violently, but a punch to the right kidney weakened his resolve and then his face was in the fish-tank again. Harry pushed upwards against Tiny's beefy hand as hard as he could, then shut his eyes as his prize fish's barbs pierced his skin.

This time, as Tiny heaved Harry up, the scorpion fish came out with the postman, its spines embedded in Harry's cheek. Harry spluttered, gurgled, then screamed in agony as the poison pumped from the fish's spines into his face. Tiny let go in surprise, and Harry slumped to the floor, clawing at his face, then screaming some more, as he succeeded merely in pricking his fingers and pushing the fish and its barbs deeper into his flesh. The toxin coursed through Harry's bloodstream and started to send his muscles into paralysis. Harry's screams turned to wheezing as he fought to get oxygen into his seizing lungs.

"What's up with him?" Tiny turned to Frank, a quizzical expression on his bull-like face. Just then, Frank's mobile phone rang.

"It's the boss," Frank said, then pressed the accept button. Tiny gave a decent impression of watching a Wimbledon Centre Court tennis match as his eyes flicked between the writhing postman and Frank, who was starting to look distinctly crestfallen.

"What is it?" Tiny asked finally, as Frank apologised to their boss for the tenth time before hanging up.

"We got the wrong house."

"What?"

"We got the wrong house," Frank hissed loudly, annoyed at having to repeat himself – an action that just seemed to emphasise the stupidity of his mistake.

"What?"

"Elgin Avenue!" yelled Frank. "66 Elgin *Avenue*; *not* Elgin *Road*… Okay? … Now let's get rid of him and get out of here!"

Harry didn't appear to be listening. His eyes were bulging out of his head; his injured hand felt like it was on fire, and he could no longer feel his face. His entire world had shrunk to the overwhelming task of forcing his lungs to expand and contract, one breath at a time.

"What about *that*?" asked Tiny, pointing to the scorpion fish jutting from Harry's face. The fish's gills were opening and closing rapidly, its eyes were bulging much in the same way as those of its owner, and it too was slowly losing its battle for life.

"Don't touch it," warned Frank, looking down in disgust at the spiny monstrosity protruding from the impossibly puffed up, bleeding face of the man at his feet. "I think it might be poisonous."

A few minutes later, Frank and Tiny were dragging the prostrate Harry out through the back door. Darkness had fallen fully during their erroneous house visit, and they took advantage of it, and the evident lack of potential witnesses, to dump Harry in the canal that ran along the bottom of the hapless postman's garden.

By the time Harry hit the water, his laboured breathing had stopped. The impact with the canal dislodged the scorpion fish, and its dead body drifted down into the murky depths.

Harry's body sank slowly, the weight of his clothes pulling him down. Greyness and calm descended on the postman, but his release was not to last long.

Suddenly Harry felt a searing pain all over his body as he jolted back to life. The gaping wounds in his face, where the fish's barbs had penetrated, were pulsating with a strange life of their own, transforming and turning into flaps of skin that rose and fell. Water entered Harry through the gashes in his cheek, but, rather than drowning, Harry's body extracted oxygen from the liquid. Harry Tomlinson had grown gills – gills that were now opening and closing, oxygenating his blood and keeping him alive. Over the next half-hour, he would grow another set.

The sick-looking young man was looking even sicker as Tiny pushed his face down towards the gas-ring.

"Where is it?" demanded Frank, as he gestured to Tiny to let the youth up. "Tell me where it is, or we light the gas."

"I don't know!" Frank produced a Zippo lighter from his pocket and proceeded to light the gas, as the youth squirmed in Tiny's grasp. Once Frank had adjusted the flame to his satisfaction, Tiny forced the youth's head down again. A strand of his hair caught fire and he screamed loudly, tearing himself out of Tiny's clutches and running headlong through the kitchen.

"For God's sake, shut him up!" snarled Frank. "The neighbours will hear him." Tiny strode over to the youth – who had reached the sink and was trying to stick his head under the tap – and punched his lights out.

"Great," complained Frank. "Now we have to sit here and wait till he comes back round." Tiny looked nonplussed for a while, but soon perked up.

"I got an idea," he beamed with pride.

"Great," Frank did little to disguise his sarcasm, but was pleasantly surprised when Tiny filled a saucepan with water and threw it in the youth's gaunt face. The young man came to, then screamed. Tiny went to hit him again, then stopped short as he realised that the youth was staring at something behind him. The thug turned around slowly and screamed too.

The excruciating pain had receded and Harry found himself floating effortlessly in the inky canal water. Despite the murk, he could see clearly all around him: mud-coloured plants, their sparse leaves swaying in the sluggish current; small fish darting this way and that, in search of food; a drowned rusty bicycle; some animal bones; a shoe; the skeletal remains of an umbrella. And beyond all those, the battered corpse of Harry's beloved scorpion fish, tangled up in a white plastic bag.

Sadness and anger overcame Harry, replacing his confusion and fear. He made a move in the direction of his dead pet, and found that he could glide easily through the water. He looked down in surprise and found that a translucent pinkish membrane had grown between his fingers. He glanced behind him, and saw that his feet were also webbed. Just then, a strong spasm shook Harry's body. He could tell that something wasn't right with his back, and then a sharp, but brief, pain shot through his spinal column as a row of long, shiny, rainbow-coloured barbs erupted through Harry's mutating skin.

With a single deft movement of his flexible spine, Harry glided through the dank water, disentangled the scorpion fish's body from the plastic, and lifted it carefully. This time its barbs didn't pierce Harry's hard new scale-covered skin. Harry gazed at the little corpse for a while, then opened his unfamiliar hand, and let the body of his pet float gently off into the dark. His anger turned to rage and … hunger. He realised that he hadn't eaten anything for hours and, to his surprise, he knew exactly what it was that he hungered for.

66 Elgin Avenue; not Elgin Road… Okay?

The words had somehow insinuated their way into Harry's subconscious and now surfaced, reverberating in his head as he navigated his way along the canals. In his eight years as postman, he'd learned all the streets in the local area and knew them – and the canals that crossed them – like the back of his hand … better than the back of his hand, as his hand was now a thing of wonder: new and strange.

Harry reached the canal that flowed parallel to Elgin Avenue and crawled out of the water. He felt a little unsteady, and it was a couple of minutes before breathing through his mouth came naturally once more. He looked around to make sure there was no one about, and headed for Number 66; anger and hunger hastening his steps.

It was late by now, and cold, and the streets were deserted, bar a black cat that hissed at Harry from a garden fence before fleeing into the shadows. Harry reached his destination and, finding the door unlocked, let himself in silently. The two pet-murderers were already there: Tiny torturing some junkie by the stove, and Frank looking on, his back to the new arrival and blissfully ignorant of what lay in store.

The scaly, spiny thing that was once the local postman crept up soundlessly behind Frank and with one deft movement ripped off his head. Blood spurted as high as the ceiling and the creature fell upon the headless corpse, sucking and tearing; its fine new set of razor-sharp teeth the perfect tool to facilitate satiation of its voracious appetite.

Tiny was too preoccupied with filling the saucepan with water and tipping it over the youth to notice anything untoward. But as soon as the young man regained consciousness, his eyes alighted on the bizarre scene that was enfolding behind the thug who'd just drenched him. As his brain worked out what his eyes were looking at, the youth started to scream. Tiny eventually followed his gaze and dropped the saucepan in horror. The sharp sound of the pan hitting the floor distracted Harry temporarily from his feeding frenzy. He saw Tiny beginning to back away, and felt himself bristle as the barbs that grew out of his back and limbs stood upright, venom pumping into them all the way to their tips.

Tiny raced for the back door, but found it locked, with no key in sight. He whipped round, saw a space between the creature and the front door, and went for it. The thing was faster; it intercepted Tiny and flung out its arm, spines first. Tiny winced as a giant barb pierced his shoulder. The creature held the thug at arm's length, watching him flap his arms around like an impaled insect. After a while Tiny started to wheeze as his throat began to constrict in reaction to the venom. As Harry delayed the coming gastronomic pleasure and watched his prey squirming before him, the junkie took the opportunity to slip past the blood-curdling scene and out through the front door. Harry let him go. Then, hungry once more, he hurled his second course off his barb and resumed his feast.

Harry found, much to his interest, that if he took his time, he was able to eat almost twice his own body weight. At about the time he was done, and all that was left of Frank and Tiny was a pile of bloody clothes, a couple of skeletons, a gun, a switchblade and two mobile phones – and about the time that the local junkie was being locked up in a holding cell after bursting into the police station, ranting about man-eating fish-monsters –

Frank's mobile rang. Harry picked it up carefully and inspected the flashing display. 'Boss' it said. Harry accepted the call.

"You done yet?" asked the surprisingly squeaky voice at the other end. Harry grunted something akin to an affirmation. "You got the stuff?" Harry grunted again. "Well why the fuck didn't you call me?" the squeaky voice at the other end rose a tone or two in apparent annoyance. Harry risked a third grunt. "Look, just get your asses down to the parking lot behind Sainsbury's. And I mean *now!*"

Harry grinned to himself and headed back to the canal. If he swam, he'd make it to Sainsbury's in five minutes. Maybe later he'd take the canals to the river, then head downriver for a mile or so. There was a prison for violent offenders downriver. Harry hated murderers and rapists. Besides, he figured he might be hungry again before daybreak.

BUY A GOAT FOR CHRISTMAS

As soon as Pierre saw the tank, he fell madly in love with it. It was large and chunky, its rotting green paint barely covering the blood-coloured flecks of rust beneath. Pierre ran his hand over the gun barrel, wincing as he caught his finger on a sliver of flaking paint. He sucked his bleeding finger and ran his other hand over the side of the tank, his eyes glowing like those of a schoolboy who's just realised that toads pop when you blow them up with a straw.

Not many people remembered the time before the war, but Pierre did. He remembered when a travelling cinema had come to the nearest town. He'd borrowed a donkey from one of his neighbours and ridden to see it. The film showing was *The Exorcist*. The other locals had walked out in protest, some of the women had fainted, and a little boy got possessed and had to be taken to the local priest after the screening. But Pierre was in seventh heaven: thrilled, terrified, moved – one emotion after another and all at once. He rode out to town every day for the three days before the cinema was closed down and the projectionist thrown out of town for blasphemy and attempting to corrupt the God-fearing locals. It was during the third and last screening that Pierre realised his life's ambition: to be able to say 'your mother sucks cocks in hell' in every language on earth. From that day on, until war broke out, he worked towards fulfilling his ambition and tried out the language skills he was acquiring on any tourist who passed through this godforsaken part of the world. Pierre often sported a black eye.

Then war broke out. Pierre's village avoided most of the violence, but hunger, poverty and disease took their toll. Now life was slowly returning to normal – the village school had re-opened, the villagers had started to rebuild their livelihoods, but they were still heavily dependent on outside help and would be for many months to come.

Mr Wyndham-Smythe of Kensington had broken his vow never to suffer going on the tube again, and was sitting, handkerchief held firmly over his nose and mouth, among the coughing commuters and excited tourists, when he noticed the Giftaid poster directly opposite him. He had already read all the other posters – twice – but somehow this one had eluded his gaze, perhaps – as is often the case in life – by merit of being directly in front of him.

'That's the family and its conscience taken care of,' it proclaimed. 'Buy a goat or some chickens from Farm Africa for £10.' The poster went on to explain that an enterprising blacksmith could convert a decommissioned tank into 3,000 farm implements for a poor African village.

Mr Wyndham-Smythe didn't like animals, particularly smelly farmyard animals tended to by dirty farmers. He found weapons and militaria much more appealing. Ever since his father had sent him to military academy and he had met Dick, the young Wyndham-Smythe was fascinated by all things military. Dick had humiliated him, played practical jokes on him, beaten him and urinated on him, and Wyndham-Smythe had loved every miserable minute. As old memories came flooding back, Mr Wyndham-Smythe reflected on his life, and his thoughts turned to his children, William and Henrietta. Henrietta had been pestering him all year for a Sony widescreen laptop with 32X Re-write DVD drive, and all William could talk about was an X-box. Well ... not this year. This year William and Henrietta would learn about the true spirit of Christmas.

"Pierre? ... Pierre!" The blacksmith had been daydreaming: imagining himself driving through the village in his perfectly polished, shining silver tank, the other villagers eyeing him with admiration and cheering as he passed. Now the village elder's voice brought Pierre out of his reveries.

"Huh?" Pierre took his hand off the tank and looked around, slightly dazed. The village elder had called all the villagers together for an impromptu ceremony in honour of the aid workers who had delivered the village's allocation of western aid and the donors who had funded the gifts.

"I said that you," the village elder told Pierre, "as the village blacksmith, will be honoured to make tools out of the old tank, so that we will be able to till our land again and grow our own crops."

"Huh?"

The village elder frowned at Pierre and turned back to the villagers, the aid workers and the two truck drivers who had convoyed in the tank, rice and farm animals.

"On behalf of everyone in the village of Santa Maria Illuminosa Madre di Jesu Crucifixio, I would like to thank the Giftaid Foundation and all of you for bringing us help in our hour of need. We also extend our thanks to the people of Great Britain, in particular to Mrs Jameson of Shepherd's Bush for the goat, Mr Thompson of Aberdeen for the chickens, and to Mr Wyndham-Smythe of Kensington and his family for the tank."

"Mr Wyndham-Smythe of Kensington," mouthed Pierre.

The village elder's speech went on for some time and Alicia was starting to feel nauseous again. She hadn't been right since the incident in Utar Pradesh. It had been dark and the aid truck she was travelling in hit what she and the driver initially thought was a large black dog. Alicia got out of the truck to see if it was still alive, and that was when it went for her. It all happened so fast. Alicia saw the creature's yellow eyes and large fangs as it sprang at her throat. She managed to raise a hand to defend herself, but if it hadn't been for the driver leaping out of the truck and hitting the animal with the cricket bat he kept next to his seat, it would have ripped her throat out for sure. Instead, it reeled under the blow from the bat, then glowered at the two humans and disappeared into the bushes.

"Are you alright?" cried the driver, rushing over to Alicia and helping her to her feet.

"I think so." Alicia inspected her bitten hand. The shock had not set in yet and she was surprised at how clear her head was at that moment. "But the dog might have had rabies," she told the driver calmly. "I need to get to a hospital as soon as possible."

"Yes, of course." The driver helped her back into the truck, adding quietly, "But that was no dog."

Despite what had happened in India, Alicia jumped at the chance to travel to Africa. Since her husband had left her for a woman half her age, Alicia had thrown herself completely into her charity work. She had been to India and to Thailand, but Africa had always been the one place that she really wanted to visit. That was where the starving children truly needed her, and the charity had finally given in to her nagging and allowed her to join one of the aid convoys, on the condition that she cover the cost of her own travel. Luckily she had enough of her parents' money left even after the divorce. But now that she was finally here, she was not feeling herself.

A skinny little boy caught Alicia's eye and she smiled at the child, happy that she was making a difference to his impoverished life. The boy's eyes opened wide and to Alicia's dismay he burst into tears and pulled his hand out of his mother's grip, running for the shelter of one of the ramshackle huts surrounding the dusty village square.

Alicia swooned slightly in the heat and wiped her brow. As the village elder's voice swam in and out of her consciousness, she started to notice other sounds around her: the agitated clucking of the chickens, the distant sound of a rat scurrying though the bushes, the heartbeat of the goat they had brought and which was now tethered with a piece of string held by one of the villagers. As she listened, fascinated, to the goat's beating heart, the animal turned to look at Alicia and bleated in alarm. Perhaps at that very moment the wind drifted in Alicia's direction from where the animal stood, but Alicia was surprised to find that she could smell the goat even at a distance of eight or so metres. And the smell told her that the animal was afraid. Alicia found herself salivating and wiped the corner of her mouth. She could hear the goat's heart beating faster and faster, and suddenly the animal was bucking in fear. The goat tore itself out of the grasp of the astonished peasant and in its confusion darted here and there among the villagers and their foreign visitors. As if noticing the wasteland that stretched beyond the villagers' huts, the goat bolted towards it, seemingly oblivious to the small man and the tank that stood in its way. The village elder spotted the goat's intentions and yelled at the blacksmith.

"Pierre! Grab it, don't let it get away!"

Pierre took his eyes off the tank and saw the goat heading straight for him. He waved his arms around and shouted at the terrified animal, causing it to swerve around him, straight into a couple of youths who had been forced by their parents to attend the village festivities. One of the boys threw himself nimbly on the goat and wrapped his arms around its neck, bringing it to the ground, where the villager who'd been made responsible for looking after it retrieved it and stroked its head gently, whispering in its ear until it calmed down.

The village elder concluded that it was time to wrap up the speeches for the time being, and invited the villagers and the visitors to join him for dinner later that evening. Slowly the villagers drifted chattering back to their huts, and the aid workers followed their designated hosts back to their accommodation. Only Pierre and one of the aid truck drivers remained. Jim had noticed Pierre's fascination with the old tank, and he wandered over to the blacksmith.

"Centurion Mark 3," Jim smiled at Pierre and patted the rusty tank. "Never thought I'd see one of these outside a museum. Figured they'd all been converted to Olifants or Semels in these parts."

Pierre nodded enthusiastically, happy that the driver spoke English – one of the few languages in which the blacksmith could do more than just quote lines from *The Exorcist*.

"I bet she's seen some action," continued Jim. "Korea, 'Nam … there's no telling where she's been."

Pierre was finding the lesson in world tank history a little hard to follow, but he certainly recognised a fellow enthusiast when he saw one.

"And this old girl could still do some damage." Jim was on a roll now, happy to have an eager listener who seemed to share his passion. He had retired from active duty a year or so earlier, and his new colleagues did not understand his fascination with tanks or appreciate his fine collection of tank badges, gun parts, and even shells of various shapes and sizes. Had any of the aid workers – or indeed his bosses at the transport company – known about the live tank shells he'd picked up and was now carting about in the back of the aid truck, he'd probably be spending his next holidays at Her Majesty's pleasure. "I've had a little look under the bonnet," Jim lowered his voice conspiratorially, "and, just between you and me, her cannon hasn't even been spiked."

Pierre smiled, perplexed, and decided to steer the conversation in a direction that he hoped would be a little easier to keep up with.

"You like tanks?" he asked.

"I was an engineer in the army," Jim explained. "I spent some time in tanks..."

Pierre's eyes opened wide and an excited flush spread over his face. "You know drive tank?" he asked, his childlike enthusiasm making the driver smile.

"Yes, I can drive one of these."

"You teach me?"

"I don't know if that's such a good idea..."

"Why?" The disappointment in the little man's face affected the driver in a way he hadn't expected. There was a naivety and innocence about the blacksmith, which made Jim feel like he had given a sweet to a child, only to take it away again.

"Well, for a start we would need some diesel."

"Diesel?"

"Fuel ... for the tank to run on."

"Oh ... yes," Pierre looked crestfallen for a while, but quickly perked up. "You have?"

"Excuse me?"

"You have diesel?"

"Well, we have some in the trucks."

"We put in tank?"

"Well ..." the driver looked down at the little man and thought for a moment. "We do have considerably more than we need. I guess you could have a bit of it..."

"Oh thank you! Thank you!"

The rumbling sound split the balmy afternoon like summer thunder, waking the villagers from their siesta and bringing them out of their huts, eyes wide with fear and curiosity. The foreigners came out too, equally fearful, but less curious – the unpleasant sound nothing new to those of them who had spent time in combat zones.

"Pierre!" The village elder did nothing to disguise his anger, but the blacksmith was in no state to notice the emotions of others. He was riding high, head in the clouds, the rest of him sat firmly in the Centurion Mark 3.

"Pierre, what the devil are you doing?" Pierre responded to the elder's exclamation by waving happily. "It works!" he cried, "It works!" His smile faded as no one apart from a couple of children waved back.

"You get out of that tank right now, blacksmith! Or there will be hell to pay!" The village elder looked ready to explode.

"Okay, I'm going. I'm going."

Everyone looked on in astonishment as Pierre turned the tank around carefully and disappeared into the scrub beyond the village. That was the last they would see of him until dinner that night.

"What do you mean, you haven't started yet? You've been gone all day and the least you could have done after your performance earlier today was to start stripping it down. You may think that the planting season is a long way away, but it will be on us faster than a hyena on an abandoned antelope calf, and what will we do if we haven't got tools to till the earth with?"

They were all sitting in the large canvas dining tent specially erected for important village occasions such as this.

Pierre was taken aback by the village elder's outburst, but he wasn't giving up easily.

"We can till the earth with sticks and sharpened stones – like we did last year and the year before that. And the kind people of Europe and America have sent us plenty of grain and dried food, and food in metal tins. We don't need to destroy the tank ... you never know when the village might need it."

The village elder was speechless for a moment and turned a deep purple colour that rather worried both his foreign guests and the other villagers, who had not seen him turn this particular shade since his son had informed him that he was marrying the girl from the neighbouring village who everyone knew was most definitely not a virgin. Finally the elder spoke:

"How dare you speak for this village, and how dare you mention the people of Europe and America!? You have betrayed everybody's trust, and you insult our guests who have come a very long way to bring us the tank so that we can till our land

and feed ourselves, and not so that you can ride around in it making a spectacle of yourself!"

The foreigners had no idea what the village elder was shouting, but they could tell that the little man his anger was directed at was not going to get off lightly. Jim picked at his plate of rice distractedly, feeling guilty and uncomfortable about his role in the blacksmith's disgrace.

"Blacksmith," the elder continued, "you leave this table now, and you go and start converting that useless piece of junk into farm tools for the people to use, or I will personally cast you out of this village and make sure that you never return!"

A gasp went round the table. Pierre hung his head and stood up.

"Yes, elder," he said quietly, and headed out of the dining tent, avoiding the eyes of the others – some pitying, some indignant, but all of them fixed on him. *"Tua madre succhia cazzi nell'inferno,"* he added under his breath in Italian as he left the tent, passing through a shaft of light from the full moon as he went.

Alicia was feeling increasingly tense. The heady smells of the food set on the table before her, and of the plants and creatures outside the dining tent were making her head spin. Some unfamiliar sense was telling her that flesh might alleviate her symptoms, and she reached out, grabbing a chunk of the pungent, fatty, non-descript meat from the large bowl that had been lovingly placed in front of her and the other foreigners. Alicia sniffed at the meat suspiciously, and immediately started to drool. She took a tentative bite, then stuffed the whole chunk into her mouth and reached out for another.

One of Alicia's colleagues had been staring at her for a while before she noticed.

"What?" she asked, staring back.

"Nothing, it's just that I thought you were vegetarian."

"I was." Alicia didn't offer anything by way of an explanation, so her colleague mumbled an apologetic, "Right," and returned his attention to his own plate.

"You must excuse our blacksmith," the elder had calmed down following Pierre's departure. "He's always been a little eccentric."

Alicia devoured several helpings of the oily meat, but still she was ravenous – ravenous and nauseous at the same time. The shaft of moonlight falling into the tent had crept its way across the floor and reached the table. It now touched Alicia and bathed her in its silver radiance. As it caressed her face, Alicia's body started to tingle. Every nerve, every sinew, every cell of Alicia's body tingled and glowed; it was as though she were dissolving and merging with the moonlight. For a moment she felt at peace, but then a light breeze stirred, bringing with it the smells of the night outside – the chickens, the goat, and other, larger, sweeter-smelling prey. Her head spun, and she had to get out – had to become part of the dark outside. She hastily made her excuses and left the tent, declining her colleague's offer to escort her to her hut.

Once outside, the night hit her with all its splendour. Alicia moved soundlessly over the dusty ground, savouring the slight chill in the air now that the sun had gone down, and the sounds of insects and small animals moving around in the scrub beyond the villagers' huts. She kicked off her shoes and felt the gritty, sandy earth beneath her feet as she wandered aimlessly through the small village, marvelling at how textured the night was, how full of colours despite the unifying silver of the moonlight. How strange that all her life she had never walked in moonlight. How strange that she had built her self-worth on what others thought of her – others like her ex-husband who had sapped all her love and youth out of her, then thrown her away. How strange that she had ever cared about anything other than the night on her skin and the moon in her hair. The moon – that was when Alicia saw it – burning in the sky above the scrub, melting away her doubts and inhibitions, dissolving her thoughts and memories until the old Alicia was no more.

Eyes still turned up to the shining orb, the new Alicia pulled off her clothes and flung them aside, intending to head for the scrub, but then a mouth-watering scent made her turn back towards the village. Sweet and inviting, it drew her relentlessly to a small hut, her excitement growing with every step she took. As she neared the hut, she felt a stabbing pain as muscle and bone shifted and transformed beneath her skin. Her skin itself seemed to burn and blister, breaking out in thousands of new hair follicles, each one sprouting a tiny black hair that grew with unnatural speed. As her spinal column and limbs recreated themselves, what was once Alicia slumped into a half-crouch. The smell emanating from the hut was irresistible now. All other sensations faded away, and there was nothing but the smell of the sleeping child waiting for her. A brief and final flash of memory – of the miles she had travelled to help the starving children. Of how they'd been waiting for her, waiting for Alicia, to come for them.

"I'm coming for you," she called out to the sleeping child, her voice a low howl emanating from deep within, silencing the insects in the scrub and piercing the delicate fabric of the moonlit night.

"What in God's name...?" The village elder stopped midsentence as the bone-chilling howl came again, unfamiliar to the villagers, but a sound instinctively to be feared nonetheless.

"It sounded just like a wolf," one of aid workers finally broke the silence that had settled like a shroud upon the dining tent.

"There aren't any wolves in Africa," Jim's fellow driver responded quietly.

"Well, it sounded just like one."

As the villagers exchanged frightened glances and everyone wondered what to do next, the howling came again, this time even lower in pitch and ending in a growling, roaring sound that was wolf, but not wolf. And this time it was accompanied by a child's terrified screams – one, two, the third one cut short.

"Paulie! Paulie!" One of the local women leapt from her place at the table and ran shrieking out of the tent. Jim ran after her, followed by the village elder and the rest of the diners.

The sight that greeted them defied belief. Loping away from one of the huts was a huge creature, wolf in all but the fact that it moved on two legs. In its jaws it carried a bleeding child, gripped clumsily by the throat. The child's mother swooned for a moment into Jim's arms, then shrieked and ran at the beast. The beast lashed out with a hideous paw-hand, its long razor-sharp claws catching the woman across the throat and flinging her to the ground, where she gurgled for a moment, then bled out.

The monster threw down the dead child and confronted the crowd of humans that had spilt from the mouth of the tent. A growl-roar rose in its throat, and then it hurled itself forward, ripping, biting, tearing. The crowd scattered, villagers and foreigners running screaming for their lives. Jim ran to his truck and returned carrying a loaded revolver.

"Hey, over here!" he shouted at the creature, drawing it away from the body of a male villager it was disembowelling. As the creature ran at him, Jim discharged several bullets, each one hitting the thing point-blank in the chest. Jim's determined expression turned to one of fear as the creature kept coming at him. It hardly broke pace as it slashed the driver across the throat with its claws, veering away from the mortally wounded man to confront a couple of village youths armed with makeshift spears.

Jim fell to the ground near the scrub, clutching at his maimed throat, trying to stop his life from draining out of him. Then a hand was touching his shoulder gently, but urgently, and the driver heard a familiar voice through the pounding of blood in his ears.

"Mr Jim! Mr Jim!" Pierre crouched down in front of the driver, distress and sorrow in his eyes.

"Pierre," Jim managed to gurgle.

"Mr Jim, you hurt bad."

"Listen Pierre..." Speaking made the blood squirt out of his wound, but Jim was experienced enough to know that nothing would save him now anyway. "Told you how the tank was fired..."

"Yes, Mr Jim."

"Still can be... Ammo ... in my truck... In back ... under blanket..."

The blood was spraying out from between Jim's fingers, and his words were coming out as little more than gurgles, but Pierre's determined nod told him that somehow the blacksmith understood.

"I use them, Mr Jim. I use them." Pierre kept his hand on Jim's shoulder until the light went out in the driver's eyes, his hand dropped from his throat and the last of his blood spurted out onto the earth.

As quickly as it had appeared amongst them, the creature disappeared, loping into the scrub and trees behind the village. But everyone – everyone who was still alive, that is – knew instinctively that it was coming back.

After a hasty and half-hearted search for Alicia, the foreigners left, saying that they would send help, and taking Jim's body with them. The villagers wished that they too could leave and say that they would send help, but they had nowhere to go. Centuries of living in a war-torn country left them in little doubt that the help which the westerners would send would not arrive in time to make a jot of difference to any of them, so they buried their dead and made plans for surviving the following night.

Alicia had fed well the previous night, but now the hunger was back, stronger than ever. She could smell the goat as though it were standing right in front of her, but she could smell the humans too – despite their best efforts to hide themselves away. She would have them all – the goat and the humans – and then the hunger would subside and she would be able to rejoice in the night and the light of the moon before it waned again to nothing.

As she approached the village, the enticing smells intensified and Alicia began to drool. She quickened her pace, the hunger inside her lesser only than the rage that accompanied it.

She burst out of the scrub and threw herself at the goat tethered to a stake in the middle of the village square. Just then something long and thin glanced off her side and fell to the ground next to her – it was a wooden spear with a sharpened stone tip, thrown by one of the villagers. Alicia roared and leapt at the man, her fangs ripping out his throat before he had a chance to scream. The other humans were all around her – pelting her with stones, spears, clubs and anything else they had managed to assemble in the way of weaponry. Alicia hardly felt a thing as the puny projectiles bounced off her thick hide. But then there was a small sting – like a mosquito bite – on her back. She spun round and saw the village elder pointing a revolver at her – one of the youths had found it lying next to the body of the dead truck driver and the elder had taken it upon himself to pull a couple of rounds of ammunition out of the dead man's pocket. Alicia felt a couple more mosquito bites as the man discharged the remaining bullets at her chest. She roared and was about to leap at him, but stopped as a loud rumbling sound caught her attention.

The creature spun round, its slanted yellow eyes staring into the scrub. Despite their terror, the villagers momentarily lowered their weapons, following the creature's gaze.

The rumbling sound grew louder and then a long metal tube broke through the brush, followed by the rest of the vehicle. The tank emerged fully from the bushes, gun barrel loaded and pointing dead ahead. The vehicle came to a halt, the lid in its top opened and the village blacksmith stuck his head out.

"Pierre!" cried the village elder, drawing the creature's attention back to himself. It growled and once more prepared to leap, but Pierre shouted as loud as he could over the rumble of the tank, "Here, over here!"

The creature turned back to Pierre and sprinted towards the tank.

"Run!" shouted Pierre. "Everybody run!"

The villagers scattered in all directions, running as fast as they could away from the village square. As the creature ran towards him, Pierre shouted at the top of his voice, "Your mother sucks cocks in hell!" Then he fired.

There was an ear-splitting noise, a bright flash pierced the darkness, and then blood and guts, fur and brain tissue, bone fragments and mucus showered all over the village square as the creature exploded into a million tiny pieces.

The months passed and the villagers tilled their land with sticks and stones, and ate the grain and dried food and tinned goods donated by the kind people of Europe and America. They did not look forward to the next convoy of Western aid, but they were ready for it.

In the lazy sunshine, a little man happily hummed Mike Oldfield's *Tubular Bells* as he polished a large gleaming silver tank.

There was talk that the village elder might allow a travelling cinema to come to the village.

CUT!

"I want her!" shouted Eli, and he wasn't going to take no for an answer – especially not from the squat, balding little runt who was the producer of this picture.

"She's a psychopath," Mark explained patiently, with the tone of one speaking to a spoilt child prone to temper tantrums. "She beat the crap out of one of the other actresses at the audition. You know she did."

"I don't care!" Eli was used to getting his own way. He was an award-winning director and, even though Hollywood was temporarily boycotting him after he caused an A-list actress to storm off the set of *Pretty Woman 2* in tears, he still pulled in a large audience, and Mark knew he was lucky to have him. This was Mark's first production. He'd made his money in IT, when that was still possible, but he'd always loved movies – and horror movies in particular – and his dream of being a film producer was finally coming true. But first he had to deal with Eli's latest whim.

"Eli, I bow to your superior experience," he said in his best calm, steady voice, "but even I know that your female lead needs to be able to act."

"You don't know shit!" Eli raved theatrically, his performance as usual over the top and such that Mark couldn't tell whether he was being serious or not. "She doesn't need to act – she's a natural! What better actress to play a psychopath than one with innate psychopathic tendencies?"

"She has no acting experience to speak of."

"She has life experience… She's perfect!" Eli was like a force of nature, and Mark didn't stand a chance.

Two weeks later and Eli's rehearsals with the actors were in full swing.

"Where's Sylvia?" asked Mark, throwing down his jacket and perching on a hard-backed chair in the small auditorium that had been hired for Eli and the actors to get together and read through key scenes in the script.

"Ah, the producer drops by!" boomed Eli in an amicable manner that immediately aroused Mark's suspicions. "Ten minutes' break, everyone!" Eli told the actors and stood up.

"Don't stop on my account," protested Mark, but it was too late.

"Nonsense!" Eli strode over to the young producer and went to put an arm around his shoulders. "Come and say hi to the talent!"

"Eli, where's Sylvia?" Mark stood his ground and Eli lowered his arm.

"Not here, dear boy." Was that a hint of sheepishness under Eli's bombastic tones? Mark thought that it was.

"Yes, I can see that she's not here. But where is she?"

"Who knows? Who cares?" Eli tried to herd Mark over to the actors, who were helping themselves to the refreshments thoughtfully provided by a production assistant, and eyeing the producer and director with growing interest. "She's probably off somewhere being Sylvia... How have you been, old boy?"

"*I* care, Eli. If I'm not wrong, you're meant to be rehearsing the car park scene today, and, if so, then I'd like to know why Sylvia isn't here." Mark wasn't going to let this go, and Eli didn't want a scene in front of the actors. The situation called for some quick thinking.

"Look," he whispered conspiratorially, pulling the producer to one side. "I'm trying out this new technique with Sylvia. Rather than over-rehearsing her to death, I've decided to play to her major strength – her spontaneity. She's at home, learning her lines, and when she finally meets the other actors on set it will be a shock for all of them – a positive, constructive shock. She'll act spontaneously, naturally, eliciting a more spontaneous and natural response from the others."

"No rehearsals for Sylvia?"

"None whatsoever!" Eli cried triumphantly, but Mark was unimpressed.

"Let me get this straight: not only have you cast an inexperienced actress as one of the leads, you are not rehearsing her until we get on set?"

"You're smarter than you look," quipped Eli. Mark ignored him.

"Eli, this isn't *Shadow of the Vampire*. You're not F. W. Murnau. And Sylvia isn't Max Schreck who needs to be kept off set to stop him eating the other cast members before the camera rolls. This is real life. We have investors whose money we're spending, and whose money I have promised to make back for them, with profit."

"Ah! Investors, money, profit, and a very amusing and apt film reference," Eli took a firm hold of Mark's arm and steered him towards the waiting thespians. "You'll make a fine film producer, mark my words ... Mark! ... but you must learn one thing – faith. Have a little faith... Now come and say hi to Tania, she's been asking lots of questions about you. If you play your cards right…"

"Put the boom down, Wendy!" Bob the boom operator was entertaining the runners with his Jack Nicholson impersonation.

"Who's Wendy?" asked Nicki. It was the pretty seventeen-year-old's first film shoot and she was grateful that the other crew members were making her feel welcome and helping her learn the ropes. The lighting guys were setting up the lights for the next scene, under the watchful eye of Graham – the Director of Photography, while the sound guys and the two runners hung out by the table with the tea, coffee and chocolate bars.

"She's Jack's wife in *The Shining*," Marty the sound recordist explained helpfully. "Put the bat down, Wendy! … Remember?" Nicki shook her head. "I'm not going to hurt you; I'm just going to bash your brains in…?"

"I haven't seen it," admitted Nicki, then added, "What's a boom?" A moment later she jumped as something large and furry touched her ear – it was Bob's long microphone pole, the mike at the end of it holstered in a fluffy grey cover, designed to reduce wind-noise during outdoor filming.

"*That's* a boom," laughed Bob, tickling Nicki with the microphone cover, then poking her in the leg with it and barking like a dog.

"Nicki, can you see if Sylvia's here yet." Andrea – the First Assistant Director – had heard Bob's Jack Nicholson impersonation a dozen times already and all of the sound guys' jokes at least as often. How predictable they were – sniffing like dogs around every pretty new runner or production assistant who wandered on set. And Nicki's long, peroxide-blonde hair and skinny girlish figure were distracting all the male technicians and rendering them even more stupid than usual. How was Andrea supposed to run a tight set under these conditions?

"Oh, okay." Nicki hadn't heard the First Assistant Director come up behind her, and Andrea took her surprised expression to be the result of being asked to actually do some work.

"Today, please, Nicki." Andrea turned to go.

"Where should I look for her?" Nicki called after Andrea.

"Start with Wardrobe, then check Make-up and Catering."

"Oh, okay." Nicki set off to look for Sylvia and the guys watched her go. Andrea huffed silently to herself and stomped off next door to make sure the Lighting Department weren't slacking.

After twenty minutes of running around the film unit, Nicki was forced to admit defeat to Andrea, and Andrea was forced to tell the director that his lead actress had failed to turn up for their first shooting day.

"Why didn't you send a car to pick her up?" demanded Eli.

"She insisted that she'd get here herself."

"Well, why don't you phone her and find out where she is?"

"We've already tried, Eli. She's not picking up at home and her mobile's off."

"Blasted woman," Eli was quick to anger and quick to come up with a solution. "Okay, we'll do the reverse shots with Clive. Then, if Sylvia still isn't here, we'll shoot some cutaways. Tell Graham that we're shooting tight first, towards the far wall with the large cabinet. Tell him he has five minutes to move the lights; that way it'll take him ten. And tell one of the runners to keep trying to get hold of Sylvia."

"Yes, Eli."

Ten minutes later, the lighting guys had finished re-setting the lights, and a disgruntled Graham was sitting next to Eli in front of the video monitor that showed what the camera was seeing. Graham checked for flares of light, double-shadows and any other lighting imperfections. Eli watched as Clive – Sylvia's acting partner in this scene – did a quick walk-through with Jamie the runner, who was standing in for the missing actress. The camera operator kept the camera focused on Clive, while Bob and Marty worked out how close they could get the microphone to the actor without the boom getting into shot. Behind Graham and Eli hovered the make-up girl, watching for any untoward shine on Clive's nose caused by reflected light from the bright film lamps.

Happy with Clive's performance, Eli decided not to waste any time.

"Ready everyone?" he asked. Nods all round. "Call it, please, Andrea."

"Quiet please everyone, we're going for a take!" Silence fell and the air buzzed with anticipation. Andrea glanced at Eli and got the almost imperceptible tilt of his head she was after. She took a deep breath, looked at the sound recordist, then added, "Roll sound!"

Marty hit record. "Rolling," he declared.

Andrea turned to the camera operator. "Roll camera!"

The operator got the old 35 mm camera running. "Speed." The concentration on set was almost tangible.

"And *action!*" Eli's authoritative voice cut through the tension, his sharp blue eyes flitting between Clive's image on the monitor and the actor himself. Then...

"Hello everyone!" Sylvia burst into the room; a flustered, red-faced Nicki hot on her heals. Clive, who'd been about to deliver his first line, almost fell over as he turned to face the door. Everyone else followed his gaze.

"Cut!" yelled Eli. "What the *hell* is *this?*" The director looked like he was about to explode as Sylvia marched onto centre stage.

"I'm sorry! I tried to stop her!" Nicki burst into tears as the First Assistant Director strode towards her angrily.

"Sylvia! What the hell are you doing?" shouted Eli.

"Sorry I'm late, Eli," responded Sylvia, not sounding sorry at all.

"You never, *never* burst onto set when we're rolling!"

"Yeah, whatever," Sylvia smoothed down her frizzy hair in a nonchalant gesture, while Eli turned to Andrea, who was telling Nicki off in a corner of the room.

"This is meant to be a secure set. Who was on crowd control?"

"Nicki."

"I'm sorry," sobbed the runner, mascara running down her face. "I tried to stop her, but, but..." Eli had already turned his attention back to Sylvia as Nicki added quietly, "she bit me."

"And you *never* turn up on set late!"

"Alright, keep your hair on, mate!" the tall and imposing Sylvia glared at Eli defiantly. The silence was total, as all eyes turned to the director, awaiting the inevitable eruption of rage that would bury them all. You could have heard the proverbial pin drop as Eli and Sylvia faced each other across the room for three very long seconds. The two of them would not have looked out of place on the set of a Western. But as usual Eli surprised everyone.

"Yes, well," he said in a calm, matter-of-fact voice. "Let's *all* keep our hair on, shall we? Now Sylvia, be a dear and get yourself off to Hair and Make-up, will you? Quick as you can. Nicki will show you where to go."

"Yes, Eli." And Sylvia went, baring her teeth at the snivelling Nicki on her way out.

"Ready to go again?" asked Eli, a demure smile on his face. His eyes dared anyone to so much as exhale loudly.

"So what happened?" Mark had popped in during the brief tea break to check on his investment.

"What do you mean, what happened?" asked Eli defensively.

"I hear you're having trouble with Sylvia."

"Oh, you hear, do you?" Mark couldn't tell whether Eli's indignation was real or fake. "You hear through your little spy network? Didn't take them long to infiltrate my set! So who was the little bird who flew to Daddy and told tales on big bad Eli?"

"Calm down, Eli. I just heard that Sylvia was late and burst in on your first shot."

"My, what precise little spies you have, my dear Mark! ... So she was late. So it won't happen again. Alright?"

"Have you shot anything with her yet?"

"Haven't you got some accounts to do or something?"

"I'm just asking what you've shot so far."

"We did Clive's singles and the cutaways. We're shooting with Sylvia next."

"Thank you, Eli."

"You're welcome, Mark. Now if you're through interrogating me, I have a film to shoot."

"Any problems, let me know. I'm here to help you, you know."

"A helpful producer, that'll be a first... Andrea! Can we get everyone together please?"

A few minutes later the required crew members filed into the room.

"Good God, man, what happened to you?" Eli enquired of Bob, who slinked in sheepishly, carrying his boom and sporting a fresh black eye.

"Nothing."

"Come now, unless you walked into your own boom, I would say that *something* happened."

"Sylvia..."

"Ah, Sylvia! Really?" Eli laughed. "And what did you do to provoke her?" No response. "Tell me!"

"She didn't like my Jack Nicholson impersonation." Bob admitted quietly.

"Aha! And to think I doubted her good taste... Speak of the devil!" Eli got up and walked over to Sylvia, who'd just entered the room. "Come on in, my dear, we'll do a walk-through."

"What?" asked Sylvia suspiciously.

"We'll walk through the scene." Eli explained. "Just don't give me a black eye; I'm not the boom operator."

"He's a prick," Sylvia growled.

"Now, now, children, play nice... Andrea! Call a rehearsal, please!"

"Hold it like you mean it!"

"What?"

"The machete! Hold it like you mean it!" They'd been rehearsing for almost an hour and the camera still wasn't rolling. Eli was beginning to lose his patience and Sylvia was getting increasingly agitated – to the point where she could no longer remember the couple of lines she'd been reciting in a startlingly wooden and inappropriate fashion when they'd first started.

"But it's not real!"

"Of course it's not real. It's a prop!" Eli was flabbergasted, and relieved that Mark had gone back to the production office and was not here to witness their disastrous walk-through.

"How can I hold it like I mean it if it's not real?"

"It's called acting," the Director of Photography hissed under his breath, loud enough for Sylvia to hear.

"You fuck!" Sylvia glowered at Graham, her face reddening with rage. Eli could swear that the woman's already frizzy hair was standing on end like that on an enraged, bristling cat.

"Good!" he bellowed. "Now use that anger, grab the machete and go for Clive." Clive looked at Eli pleadingly, his eyes those of a startled deer. Sylvia made a move towards the plastic machete. "Wait!" shouted Eli. "Wait for Andrea to call it! We'll go for a take... Andrea!"

"Quiet please, we're going for a..." But it was too late. Screaming like a banshee, Sylvia grabbed the machete and ran.

"Roll camera!" Eli managed to shout, but Sylvia raced past the cowering Clive and headed straight for the Director of Photography, knocking over the monitor in the process. The camera operator tried to pan the camera after Sylvia, while Graham raised his arms to fend off the attack, yelling for someone to get her off him. Andrea ran at Sylvia, but Eli stayed her with a hand gesture. He watched with keen interest for a couple of seconds as Sylvia pelted the Director of Photography with the plastic prop, before finally relenting.

"Cut!" he shouted. Sylvia stopped – the result of running out of steam rather than anything Eli had said. "Good!" cried Eli. Graham stormed out of the room, cursing. The remaining crew stood in stunned silence.

"Put the prop down, Wendy," Marty whispered to Bob, with a dry smile. Eli came up to Sylvia, removed the machete from her hand and led her to the side.

"That wasn't bad," he told her. But I have two directions for you. One: you wait until I say 'Action!' And two: Clive..." Clive glanced over on hearing his name, his face positively ashen. "You go for Clive – your fellow actor, not for my Director of

Photography. Other than that, you do everything the same. Do you understand?"

"Yes, Eli."

"Good... Andrea!" The First A.D. turned her attention away from the monitor that the camera assistant had managed to reconnect.

"Yes, Eli?"

"Get someone to fetch the Director of Photography and then call a take."

"No, no, no! *No!*" Eli leapt from his director's chair. "What did I tell you?"

"What?" barked Sylvia.

"I told you to do everything the same as before!"

"I am!"

"No, you're not! You're not waiting until I say 'Action!' and you're holding it like it's a limp kipper... Here, look..." Eli took the prop from Sylvia and acted out the scene with Clive. "That's how you do it... Do you think you can do that, Sylvia?"

"Yes, Eli." Eli was making her look bad in front of the crew and Sylvia was feeling increasingly resentful. Normally she wouldn't let anyone talk to her like that, but there was something about the man that made her – and everyone else on set, it seemed – want to please him. Sylvia figured it must be something to do with being the Director. Nevertheless, she just couldn't see what all the fuss was about. She was doing what Eli told her – most of it, at any rate. Okay, so sometimes she forgot to wait until he said 'Action', but she was waving the pathetic plastic machete at Clive, so what was the problem?

Minutes went by, then hours. Then it was time for lunch. As usual, the caterers put on a good spread. Sylvia followed the others to the catering van, then took her tray onto the coach that had been turned into a mobile dining room, complete with tables and seats. She was convinced that the crew were giving her funny looks. And she could swear that even that gay-looking pathetic piece of shit Clive – or whatever his stupid name was – smirked at her as she walked past. She wondered how fast that smirk would disappear if she stuck his head down the portable toilet – or 'honeywagon' as it seemed to be called around here. Eventually she found an empty table in the corner and settled down to her three-course meal, glaring at anyone who ventured close.

"*Bon appétit*, everyone!" Eli had entered the coach with Graham. He spotted Sylvia sitting by herself, murmured something to the Director of Photography, then came over to the actress.

"Mind if I join you?" he asked, sitting down.

Sylvia shrugged, not bothering to look up from her plate.

"Look, Sylvia, the first day of shooting is always the hardest." Eli was doing his caring, empathetic director routine again, and Sylvia cast him a cynical glance. "Once we've all eaten, everyone will be in a better mood, it'll be easier to concentrate and everything will be fine. You'll see. You just need to follow my directions to the letter and everything will be okay."

But everything wasn't okay. Eli tried to be patient, taking Sylvia to the side and calmly repeating over and over what she needed to do. But nothing worked. Sylvia's acting went from very bad to atrocious; she came in at the wrong times, fluffed her lines, dropped the machete and was unable to follow the simplest instructions. What's more she didn't seem to care, and it was her attitude more than anything that was driving Eli to distraction.

"Am I speaking English?" he finally burst out. It was six p.m. and they still didn't have any useable takes. "What is it that I'm saying that you don't understand? How can you call yourself an actress if you can't follow directions?"

"Oh, fuck off, you stupid old fruit!" And that was it. Eli sacked his leading lady in front of the entire crew. Sylvia let off a tirade of obscenities at the director, then stormed off set, pushing aside anyone who didn't move out of her way fast enough.

Eli returned home exhausted and humbled. He'd had to swallow a whole lot of pride where Mark was concerned. After they'd wrapped for the day, with footage in the can which came to a shocking total of probably no more than one screen minute, Eli had had to phone the producer, apologise for his lack of judgement and ask Mark to help him re-cast the female lead. Luckily Mark had behaved like a gent.

"Of course," he'd said with a logic-defying lack of smugness that Eli appreciated greatly at that particular point in time. The young producer had then taken Eli back to his place, where he'd fixed him a stiff drink, and the two of them had sat together for four hours, reviewing the audition tapes until they'd picked out an actress they could both live with.

"I'll phone her straight away," Mark told Eli.

"Thanks, old boy," Eli relaxed into Mark's leather sofa and took a sip of Scotch.

"I'll just get the casting file and check her number."

Fortunately, not only was the actress still available, but she agreed to learn the minimum-dialogue scene that Sylvia had massacred – overnight – and start work the next day.

"I'm having the script couriered to her right now. She'll be in first thing in the morning and we won't even have to rearrange the shooting schedule."

"A helpful producer," Eli raised his glass to Mark and smiled at the younger man. "That'll be a first."

Mark had called him a cab and Eli staggered up to his front door, a little drunk, but relieved that with Mark's help he'd be able to save face in front of the crew. Tomorrow he'd act as though Sylvia had never even existed, and everyone would follow suit. Perhaps Graham would make some snide little remark, but that was Directors of Photography for you – an inflated sense of self-importance, the lot of them.

Eli took out his house keys, and that's when he noticed that the front door was open. His usual astuteness dulled by the whisky he'd had at Mark's, he simply put his keys back in his pocket and went in, shutting the door behind him.

"Honey, you left the front door open," he called, looking around for his wife. "You should be more careful, you know." Getting no response, he assumed that she'd already gone up to bed, and padded over to the fridge to get himself a beer. There he stood stock still for a while, as his brain grappled to work out what it was that his eyes were looking at. His mouth opened in a scream, but the scream was totally silent. Finally Eli backed away from the open fridge, spun round, clipped his side on a worktop, fell over and hit his head. When he regained consciousness, Sylvia was standing over him with a meat cleaver.

Again Eli tried to scream, and again found that he couldn't make a sound. Too shocked to get up, he backed away from the looming apparition – on his backside, his mouth opening and closing like a fish out of water. He tried to cry out for help, and couldn't for the life of him understand why his vocal cords wouldn't oblige. And then the weirdest memory sparked in his brain. Eli had once filmed an interview with an old man who'd been a British spy during World War II. Once they'd finished shooting, Eli had commented on how brave the man was, and how he was sure that he himself would blab under torture within a couple of seconds.

"You don't know that, son," the man had told Eli, gazing benevolently at the young director through rheumy eyes. "Sometimes you just freeze up and you can't say anything, even if you want to. You never know how you'll react in a given situation until you're in it." And now Eli finally realised what the old man had meant. But nobody was going to give him a medal for it.

"I'm sorry, Eli!" Sylvia took a step forward and Eli nearly pissed himself. "I didn't mean what I said today. You're not an old fruit, and you're right: I *can* do better." Eli threw a devastated glance in the direction of the fridge; any doubts that he really *had* seen his wife's decapitated head stuffed in between yesterday's pot-roast and the cauliflower dispelled by the presence of the homicidal maniac now towering above him. Sylvia followed his gaze. "Oh ... her? She wouldn't let me in. I tried to explain that I needed to talk to you; to straighten things out. But she wouldn't listen. She told me to get out, and she just went on and on. What a bitch! I don't know how you put up with her, I really don't." Sylvia was getting worked up and Eli almost started hyperventilating in his ineffective effort to scream for help. "I did you a favour, you know. You should be grateful. You should take me back, you know. I can do better. You said if I follow all your directions to the letter, everything will be okay."

Speechless still, Eli continued to inch backwards on his buttocks, feeling his way behind him with his hands. He winced as wooden splinters broke off in his fingers, and regretted having ignored his wife's entreaties to sand and polish the floor.

"*Look*, Eli!" The longer the director was unable to speak, the more desperate the actress became to elicit a response. "Look! I *can* act! I'll prove it to you!" she cried, brandishing the meat cleaver in a manner that could only be construed as threatening. "I'm acting ... see? I'm holding it like it's real ... see? I just want another chance. I just want you to take me back!" Tears rolled down Eli's face. He gasped as he felt the wall behind him. He had run out of floor space; he could back no further. Sylvia cornered him, the meat cleaver raised high above her head. "I'm acting ... see? I'm following your directions ... see? I'll do whatever you say! Just tell me what you want me to do, Eli! Just tell me!"

Eli was close to choking in his attempts to cry out; to make the whole nightmare that was Sylvia go away ... to articulate the one word that would make her stop.

"Tell me!" screamed Sylvia.

"Cut!" whimpered the director. Sylvia cut.

ARTHUR'S CELLAR

Arthur raced through the darkening forest, ignoring the branches that scratched him and the roots that tried to trip him as he ran. But it wasn't a root that caused him to fall flat on his face – it was something soft and wet, which gave underfoot, but offered just enough resistance to send Arthur sprawling.

"Sonofabitch!" Arthur cursed loudly, rubbing his swollen ankle and studying the dead rabbit closely. The blood was only just congealing in its empty eye sockets and it still retained a remnant of body heat. Arthur sighed and pulled himself to his feet, surveying the surrounding woods. The creature couldn't have got far. It was old and almost blind, its muscles surely atrophied by years of confinement. But despite its age and poor physical condition, the beast was still dangerous.

Just then a twig snapped behind Arthur. Startled, the young man cocked his rifle and pointed it in the direction of the sound. Silence. Then a scuffling noise off to the left. Arthur panicked and shot into the bushes. A flurry of wings as a startled bird took off into the sky. Arthur's shoulders slumped with relief, but he knew that the evening was far from over. He looked down at the mutilated rabbit and spotted a broken branch nearby; this gave him the clue he needed to ascertain the direction that the creature had taken.

Arthur had been five years old when he first became aware that something was not right in his grandfather's house. Sometimes there were noises at night. Low shuffling sounds, moaning, wailing. Arthur's grandfather had explained that there was a monster in the cellar. Arthur burst into tears and his grandfather comforted him and assured him that the monster could not harm him because it was locked up securely. Arthur asked why grandfather didn't kill it, and the old man explained that it was wrong to kill and that the monster would eventually die on its own. It was grandfather's duty to guard the monster, and one day it would be Arthur's job.

"I don't want to guard the monster!" Arthur shook his head firmly. His grandfather laughed and said not to worry – he would try to live a long time, to carry out his duty as long as possible.

Arthur's grandfather had kept his word. He was ninety-three now, and more determined than ever to outlive the creature. But his grandfather was growing progressively more frail, and it was up to Arthur now to feed the thing and see to its basic needs while it still breathed.

Arthur remembered the first time he had seen the beast. It was on his eighth birthday that his grandfather had deemed him old enough to do so. Before unlocking the cellar door, grandfather gave Arthur a long and boring history lesson about World War II.

"It was a terrible time," he told the boy. "Terrible. Suffering and death everywhere you looked... You never knew what was waiting for you around the corner." Noticing the blank expression in Arthur's eyes, Grandfather decided to get to the point. "Anyway ... one day I'd just got back from the east field, and I was going around the side of the barn, when what do you suppose I saw?" The old man's glance at his grandson was rewarded with a yawn, but he was determined to finish his story. "Right there – right in front of me – was a vile monster, a devil from hell itself." Arthur perked up, his eyes widening. "I caught it unawares – it hadn't heard me coming. Well, I wasn't about to wait for it to kill me, so I grabbed the pitchfork that was leaning against the wall and I ran it right through the fuc ..." Arthur's eyebrows arched in astonishment, but Grandfather quickly checked himself and carried on, "... the devil. I couldn't kill it because that wouldn't be Christian, but I ran it through right good, then I dragged it here and locked it up, so it could do no more harm."

The last of the light was slowly draining from the sky and Arthur was beginning to feel scared. His swollen ankle was slowing him down, and soon it would be hard to distinguish the trees from the other grey shapes in the forest.

Arthur wondered what havoc the creature could wreak if it remained at large. It must have moved pretty fast to kill the rabbit; Arthur still did not understand how something that old could move so quickly. He wondered if bloodlust – and the creature was not short of that – could have an animating effect. He still had vivid memories of the speed with which the beast had thrown itself at the man from the loan company who had come to take grandfather's telly away. Arthur was thirteen at the time.

"It's in the cellar," Grandfather had told the man.

"Excuse me?"

"The television," Grandfather peered at the man with his cold blue eyes. "It's in the cellar." The man stared at Grandfather uncomprehendingly. "I figured you might be coming for it, so I boxed it up and stored it for you in the cellar."

"I see," the man sounded like he didn't see at all.

"I'd get it for you," continued Grandfather, "but my arthritis has been playing up terribly and my knees make it very hard for me to walk down the steps... I don't suppose you'd mind getting it yourself?" There was a long pause.

"Well ..." the man said finally. "Alright."

The man had gone down into the cellar and the creature, which had been dozing in a corner, was upon him in an instant, snarling, biting and tearing. It had all been over in seconds. The other men who came – men from the loan company, developers who wanted to buy Grandfather's farm, and even a police officer – had all been dispatched the same way. Some took longer, some took less time, but the creature got them all in the end, and Grandfather got to keep his farm and his television set.

Yes, there was no telling how much damage the creature would do if Arthur did not succeed in getting it back to the cellar ... or killing it. He could always tell his grandfather that there had been an accident.

Just then, Arthur heard a low feral noise behind him – a kind of hungry growl, full of anticipation and barely controlled rage. He spun round to see the creature crouching by a nearby tree. Arthur's blood froze. He had never seen the creature clearly. It had always been in the half-light of the cellar, and even now it was merging into the shadows of the forest.

Arthur was a little boy again, on his eighth birthday, shaking with fear as his grandfather slowly unlocked the cellar door and let him peer into the darkness.

There was a horrifying, gurgling growl coming from the corner of the cellar. Then suddenly, a flurry of white, as a thing with a long grey beard and wisps of greasy white hair threw itself towards the stairs on which Arthur and his grandfather were standing. Arthur screamed and stumbled back, but his grandfather reassured him.

"Don't worry," he said. "It's on a chain. It can't get to us."

As Arthur watched, the creature reached the bottom of the stairs, yelped and fell, the chain cutting cruelly into its bare ankle. The black tatters of a military uniform hung loosely off its emaciated frame and the silver lightning-like SS signs on the shoulders of the creature's jacket sparkled in the meagre light from the weak light bulb overhead.

Arthur stood in horrified awe – now, as he had then. The creature growled again and started to circle Arthur in the gloom, its milky eyes used to the darkness. Arthur raised his rifle and aimed, but it was too late. The small, rank, drooling creature was upon him, the remains of its rotting teeth already sinking into the soft part of his throat, just under his chin.

THE APPRENTICE

Ralph baked bread. It was a strange feeling – using those massive, clumsy knuckles to knead the soft dough rather than to rain down the wrath of God on the head of anyone who gave him a funny look. A strange feeling to have people smile at him trustingly and talk to him about the weather while they waited for him to wrap the warm scented bread, rather than cross the road when they saw him coming. Yes, it was a piece of good fortune that Ralph had picked up a little of the trade from his mother before his father had battered her to death. And lucky too that Ralph had chanced upon the village just at the time when their baker had gone for a walk and been found beaten to a pulp by the side of the road. Not that Ralph claimed to know anything about that.

Ralph's customers were very fond of his braided loaves and animal shapes, but Ralph's real speciality – and his own particular favourite – were the little heart-shaped buns. Ralph's heart-shaped buns were the talk of the village, and people came from miles around to buy them for their sweethearts, their spouses or their children.

Ralph didn't have any children, a sweetheart or a spouse, nor did he feel any need for them. As far as he could tell, children were always wailing or causing mischief, and women were always nagging or demanding money from their long-suffering husbands. No, what Ralph really wanted was an apprentice – someone who would help out around the bakery; someone to whom Ralph could impart his knowledge, whom he could nurture, and kick the shit out of now and again when he got annoyed and needed to let off a little steam. That was what Ralph wanted. It would be kind of like playing God.

Then one day Ralph's prayers were answered. It was hard to tell the boy's age; he was slight and pale, with a mop of unruly dark hair. He could have been twenty or he could have been twelve; there was no way to find out as the boy never spoke a word. He turned up one evening, just as it was getting dark, with a sign around his neck that read, 'I will work for food and lodgings.' Not only was the boy mute, but Ralph's attempts to communicate with him by way of a quill and some parchment led the baker to believe that he couldn't read or write either. Luckily for Ralph, the boy didn't appear to be deaf, and responded to his invitation to sit down and eat by doing just that.

There was a hint of desperation in the speed with which the boy wolfed down his food, and something pitiful in the way he threw Ralph an occasional sideways glance, as if worried that the man would take the food away before he had devoured it all. Ralph felt a confusing mixture of pity and annoyance – a feeling that would grow over the coming weeks – and barely resisted the urge to tear the bowl away from the boy before he had finished eating.

After supper, Ralph took the boy to the small barn that used to house his horse – before he'd flogged it to death – and told the boy that he could sleep there and start work the following morning. The boy looked at Ralph and nodded. And so it was that Ralph got himself an apprentice.

That night Ralph had trouble falling asleep and, when he finally did, he dreamt that he was on a scaffold, about to be executed. He was protesting his innocence, but nobody seemed to care; they just shoved a gag in his mouth and hanged him anyway. When he woke up the next morning, Ralph had a stiff neck and a splitting headache. He could still remember that terrible burning sensation of the rope biting into his neck, and he was in a foul mood. Then he remembered the boy. He strode to the barn and saw him fast asleep in the hay.

"Get up, you lazy shit!" Ralph kicked the bale of hay that the boy was lying on. The boy fell off, eyes wide with surprise, then got up and walked out of the barn, towards Ralph's house, which doubled up as the village bakery. Something about the calmness in the boy's stride annoyed the hell out of Ralph.

"Watch and learn," Ralph hissed, proceeding to mix and knead the dough for the day's bread before shaping it and placing it carefully in the large oven. When he was done with the morning's baking, he ordered the boy to clean up the bakery before the first customers arrived.

"Who's this?" Ralph's customers gazed curiously at the shy young man cowering in the corner.

"That's my new apprentice." Ralph beamed.

"Where'd he come from?"

"Oh… He's my cousin's boy."

"Never knew you had a cousin, Ralph."

"Aye, I do… She asked me to train him to be a baker."

"I see… He doesn't say much, does he?"

"No, he doesn't at that." And that's when Ralph realised the beauty of his situation. The boy would never talk back, never contradict him, never complain.

After the last of the customers had left, Ralph closed up for the day and put out two plates of food. The boy approached the table cautiously. Ralph let him sit down and reach a hand out towards the plate. "No!" he shouted, and pulled the plate away roughly. "You clean up and then you eat!"

Ralph watched the boy wipe down the work surfaces and sweep up the spilt flour. The boy was so pale and skinny. There was something unsavoury about him – unhealthy – rather like a mangy dog. When the boy got close to baker while sweeping, his back to the man, Ralph surprised both of them by kicking him. The boy sprawled on the floor, then picked himself up silently and continued sweeping. Ralph laughed. "You can eat now," he told the boy, and left the room.

The next day Ralph got up earlier than usual and was on his way to kick the boy awake, but found him already waiting on the doorstep.

"Oh, you're up." Ralph let the boy in. "In that case, you can show me what you learned yesterday about making bread." Ralph watched as the boy mixed the flour and water, and kneaded the dough carefully.

"Not like that, you have to do it harder." Ralph put his large hand over the boy's wrist, intending to help him knead the dough, but somehow the feel of that thin, cold small hand brought about the irresistible urge to crush, pulverise, destroy. He suddenly needed to hear bones crack and feel the little digits turn to jelly in his grasp. The boy winced in pain, but didn't cry out. Ralph stopped abruptly and let go of the boy's hand, wondering just how much damage he'd done, afraid that the boy might not be able to work. The boy held his limp hand, but soon moved his fingers a little, assuring Ralph that he'd stopped in time and there was no real injury.

75

"That's enough now. Go and sweep the floor." The boy did as he was told, largely using his other hand to hold the broom.

Ralph couldn't really complain about the boy's work. He kept the bakery clean, he did a good enough job with the dough and the animal shapes and even the hearts, but there was something in his manner that Ralph found irritating. Maybe it was the lack of enthusiasm. There was something amazing about making bread to feed people, but from the absence of emotion in the boy's face, Ralph was sure that he didn't feel that wonder at all. Somewhere at the back of Ralph's mind floated the notion that perhaps he could beat the wonder into the boy.

As the days passed, Ralph's customers noticed that his new apprentice seemed to have a knack for acquiring black eyes and fresh bruises on a regular basis.

"He's very clumsy," Ralph explained. "If there's a door, you can guarantee he'll walk right into it. If there's something lying on the ground, you can rest assured he'll trip over it and fall flat on his face." Ralph's customers sympathised with the baker – it must be hard for the man having such a clumsy apprentice, and it wasn't as if he could sack him, the boy being his cousin's child and all.

After three weeks of beatings, the boy's face remained emotionless. He took punishment with the same apparent stoicism as he took the extremely rare praise bestowed on him by the baker. Occasionally the boy would look at Ralph with a dispassion that drove the man to increasing acts of violence.

One evening when the boy was waiting for the bread stove to cool down so that he could clean it, Ralph grabbed him and shoved his head in the oven. The heat was insufficient to do any serious harm, but it must have hurt. The boy resisted only for the briefest moment – an instinctive reaction born of surprise, but then went totally limp in the baker's powerful arms, and Ralph was able to push him headfirst into the hot dark space.

"Scream, you fuck, scream!" shouted Ralph. But the boy didn't scream and didn't struggle. When Ralph finally pulled him out again, the boy's face was bright red, and sweat and tears were streaming down his face. The boy swooned a little, but remained standing, gazing at Ralph with what at first glance appeared to be the same blank expression he normally wore. Then for a moment, in the flicker of the candlelight, Ralph thought that the corners of the boy's mouth had turned up just a little, but no – surely it was just a trick of the light and shadows playing around the room.

"You want to act like a dumb animal, you'll be treated like a dumb animal." Ralph marched the boy to the barn and fetched an old dog chain lying in the corner. He brandished it at the boy, but the boy didn't flinch. Unnerved, Ralph chained the boy and tethered him in the barn. You never knew what was going on in that scrawny head of his. Perhaps behind that stoic facade he was hatching some elaborate escape plan. It was best to err on the side of prudence.

From that time on, Ralph chained the boy up at night, releasing him to carry out his chores during the day. He cut down on his meals too, as depriving him of food seemed to be the only thing that elicited any reaction from the boy, in the form of the slightest hint of a frown.

One day Ralph entered the barn and noticed a fetid smell, as if a rodent had died somewhere in the hay and was starting to rot. He looked around, and finally realised that the putrid stench was emanating from the boy. The metal chain had been cutting into the boy's ankle and the flesh had started to fester. Ralph understood the danger of infection, and took the boy into the house, to disinfect the wound.

As the baker swabbed the wound with alcohol, he looked at the boy's emaciated body, the bruises all over his arms and legs, and felt an unfamiliar twang of guilt. He looked up from the boy's infected ankle and saw the boy gazing at him with those dispassionate brown eyes. As had happened so many times before, rage at the boy's passivity and acceptance of his situation quickly replaced any pity the baker might have felt.

"What are you staring at?" The boy lowered his gaze, but it was too late; Ralph could feel the unstoppable fury growing inside him and he grabbed his horsewhip. By the time the red mist had cleared, Ralph realised he was still seeing red, as the boy was lying on the floor in a pool of his own blood.

"Oh my God!" For the first time since he was twelve – and had broken his father's favourite pipe – Ralph started to panic. He remembered his dream and the stinging feeling of the noose around his neck. He threw the whip into a corner and knelt beside the unconscious boy. "I'm sorry. I'm so sorry! Oh, please God don't let him be dead. Oh, please don't be dead. I'll never lay a finger on you again, I swear!" Ralph knelt beside the boy and wept.

After what seemed like a very long time, the boy coughed, fresh blood spattering from his mouth and merging with the pool on the floor.

"Thank God, thank God." Ralph wanted to carry the boy to his bed, and reached out to touch him, but thought better of it. "Stay here. Don't move. I'm going to fetch the doctor."

When Ralph got back with the doctor, the boy was quite still once more.

"Good God!" The doctor hurried over to the boy. "What happened?"

"I don't know." Ralph squirmed as the doctor eyed him suspiciously. "He's free to do what he wants on Sunday. He went off to the neighbouring village, I think, and next thing I know he staggers in and collapses. I think he was attacked." The doctor gazed at Ralph for a moment longer, then turned back to the boy, carefully examining his head, back and chest.

"He's taken a severe beating. He has broken ribs and a broken arm. If his wounds get infected, he will die." The devastated expression on Ralph's face dispelled any suspicions the doctor might have had about the baker's guilt in the boy's predicament. "He can't be transported anywhere. I'll try to make him as comfortable as I can here, and you send for his mother."

"I'll take care of him." The doctor looked at Ralph in surprise. "I mean, his little brother and sister are very sick. My cousin can't leave them. Look, just tell me what to do and I'll look after him."

Ralph nursed the boy for many weeks. He cut down his opening hours and reduced the number of orders he took in. He would get through the baking and the selling as fast as he could, then spend the rest of the day and much of the night sitting by the boy, listening to his laboured breathing and hoping that his heart wouldn't stop. But it wasn't just fear of death – should he be found guilty of the boy's murder – that so unsettled Ralph. He had taken life before, but now for the first time he felt remorse.

The boy drifted in and out of consciousness. The doctor came by regularly to check on him and bring more medicine. Customers were complaining that Ralph's little heart-shaped buns didn't taste as good as they used to – it was as if the heart had gone out of them.

Then one day, having apologised to the comatose boy a dozen times and cried himself to sleep the night before, Ralph awoke to find the boy sitting up in bed, watching him. Startled, Ralph started mumbling incoherent apologies, "Forgive me, please forgive me."

The boy dropped his gaze from Ralph's face and reached slowly and painfully for the edge of the bedclothes, pulling them off himself. Then, equally slowly and painfully, he swung his legs out of bed and tentatively put his weight on them.

Ralph looked on in amazement and trepidation as the boy got out of bed and walked stiffly across the room, to the far corner. Leaning on the wall for support, the boy bent down cautiously and retrieved something from the floor. As Ralph watched, too shocked to move, the boy came towards him, one painful step at a time. When he was right in front of the trembling baker, the boy lifted his functioning arm, holding out the object he had picked up. Ralph looked down to see the horsewhip; the boy was holding it by the whipping end, offering the handle to Ralph to grasp. As Ralph looked in horror from the whip to the boy, for the first time since he had come into Ralph's home, the apprentice's face broke out in a smile.

THE GIRL IN THE BLUE COAT

So it's our last day together. You've been a good listener. And thanks to you I'll have a voice – albeit a posthumous one... I'm sorry – I've made you feel uncomfortable. But I believe that's what you wanted to cover today – my thoughts on my imminent demise. Well, we can do that, but first I want to tell you a story. I've never told it to anyone, but then again you're not really anyone – are you? Please don't be offended – you know I value your work, and one day you'll be a successful writer in your own right and under your own name. But today you're just the extension of a dying old man.

The painkillers they're giving me have stopped working; the pain is becoming unbearable, and soon I'll be on morphine. The doctors tell me I'll be hallucinating and delusional, and nobody will believe the ranting of a cancer-ridden old man... Is the Dictaphone working? Good... As you're my ghostwriter, the story I'll tell you is most appropriate because it's a ghost story – at least, I think it is... Do I believe in them? Perhaps once you hear the story, *you'll* be able to tell *me*. I don't know. It all happened long ago...

I'd only been working at *The History Magazine* for four months, but they were pleased with my research skills, and I was the only person on the staff who spoke Polish. It was my second job since leaving university, and I'd already cut my teeth on an established, if somewhat trashy, London daily. So when the powers that be decided to revisit the Holocaust, the Senior Editor chose me to go to Poland.

I'd been to Poland before, of course. My mother's family hailed from the beautiful city of Krakow, and I'd been taken there fairly regularly as a boy to visit my aunt and cousins. But this time I was to travel to Międzyrzec – a small and unremarkable town, the name of which caused considerable hilarity among my colleagues, and which I myself could scarcely pronounce.

"You'll be going to My ... Mee ... here ..." said my boss, thrusting a piece of paper at me with a touch of good-natured annoyance at the intricacies of Polish orthography. Foreign names and places were never his thing in any case. He seemed happiest in his leather chair behind his vast desk in the *Magazine* office, and I sometimes suspected that the furthest he'd been from Blighty was Majorca, where he'd holiday with his wife and children at every given opportunity. And nothing wrong with that; nothing wrong at all – I thought – as I drove my hire car through the grey and brown Polish countryside, trying hard not to pile into any of the horse-drawn carts that occasionally pulled out in front of me without warning from some misty dirt side track.

I'd done my homework before driving the eighty miles east from Warsaw to Międzyrzec. Before the outbreak of World War II there had been about 12,000 Jews living in the town – almost three-quarters of the population. The town had synagogues, Jewish schools, Jewish shops, a Jewish theatre, two Jewish football teams, a Jewish brothel and a Jewish fire brigade. I wondered idly whether the Jewish fire brigade was sent to extinguish fires in Christian homes too, or just in Jewish ones. I figured it was the former, as by all accounts the Poles and Jews got on like a house on fire – excuse the pun – and most of the town's inhabitants worked happily side by side in a Jewish-owned factory, producing kosher pig hair brushes, which were sold as far afield as Germany. In fact, commerce in Międzyrzec flourished to the degree that the envious, poverty-stricken inhabitants of surrounding towns and villages referred to the place as 'Little America'... Does prosperity render a man better disposed towards his fellow man? I don't know. Certainly, during the course of my research I read of various acts of generosity – big and small – which were extended to others regardless of background, so that, for example, when a film such as *The Dybbuk* came to town, the cinema owner would organise a free screening for all the citizens of Międzyrzec, and the queue stretched half way down the main street.

As with any positive status quo, the good times in Międzyrzec were not to last long. When war broke out in September 1939, the town was bombed, then taken by the Germans, before being handed over to the Russians, and finally falling into German hands once more. The horrors that followed were fairly typical for Nazi-occupied Poland. The Polish population was terrorised, while the Jews were harassed, attacked, rounded up and either murdered on the spot or sealed in a ghetto, from which they were eventually shipped off to death camps. Nothing new there, I thought, as by now I was becoming – not jaded by all the atrocities I'd read about, but something of a reluctant expert on Nazi war crimes and the pattern they followed in the towns and villages of German-occupied Poland. And yet something about the destruction of this surprisingly harmonious community – not just the murder of people, but the annihilation of a functional and thriving symbiotic organism formed from thousands of disparate souls – added to the customary level of distress that I'd somehow learned to live with since being assigned to the Second World War project.

Finally the countryside gave way to ramshackle housing, and the dark green and white road sign confirmed that I'd arrived at my destination. All I had to do now was find the town library, where I had a meeting with the librarian turned amateur historian – a pleasant fellow with a neatly trimmed brown beard, who furnished me with the details of several elderly local residents, including a lady who 'remembered the War'.

"She doesn't have a telephone," he told me as I thanked him and took the piece of paper inscribed with the names and addresses, "but she's almost certain to be at home. You can't miss the house. It's the last house but one on the left as you leave town, going east. It's one of the old wooden houses, and you'd be forgiven for thinking that you'd already left Międzyrzec, as those old houses are virtually out in the countryside."

I decided to start at the far end of town, with the old lady. Everything was as my bearded friend had said: the ugly apartment blocks and equally unattractive family houses (presumably built hastily after the war to re-house those whose homes had been destroyed) gave way to what looked like small wooden farmhouses, with fields and meadows behind them stretching away into the distance.

I drove slowly in an effort to ascertain which house was the last but one on the left-hand side before leaving town. I was fairly sure it was a run-down wooden house with peeling green paint, set back from the road. I drove past just to check, but I'd been right – there was only one more house beyond the one I'd instinctively picked out. I turned the car around carefully and doubled back, pulling up on the grass verge by the side of the road. Chain-link fencing some six feet in height surrounded the property, and the only way in – from the roadside, at least – was through a gate, which was locked. There was a bell, but no intercom. I pressed the bell and waited. After a minute or so I pressed it again, not sure if it was even working.

After a couple more minutes, the front door of the house opened with a creaking worthy of an old horror movie, and an elderly grey-haired woman peered out apprehensively. I waved at her and after a moment's hesitation she waved back. Then she went back inside and shut the door behind her. I was taken aback and nearly rang the doorbell again, but then the woman reappeared, pulling a woollen shawl over her shoulders. I smiled at her reassuringly as she made her way slowly and painfully down the porch steps and across the front yard towards me.

"How can I help you?" she asked through the fencing.

"Hello, my name is Frank Johnson," I told her. "I work for *The History Magazine* in London, and I understand from Dr Lipinski that you remember the time when there was a ghetto..." I never got to finish my sentence. The old lady had been observing me with amicable curiosity, but now her face crumpled and she started sobbing uncontrollably, tears streaming down her face and gathering in her wrinkles. I was mortified and started to mumble a hasty apology, but the woman raised her hand in a conciliatory gesture.

"I'm sorry," she managed to say. "I'll take some medicine for my nerves. Please come back in an hour and I'll tell you all about the ghetto." I smiled at her as best I could and nodded my head vigorously. "The gate will be open," she added, trying unsuccessfully to stem the flow of tears with a shaky hand.

"I'll come back in an hour," I told her.

There was really nothing constructive I could do in an hour, but I didn't want to make the old lady any more uncomfortable by sitting outside her house, so I drove back into the town centre, parked up and sat in my car. There was no decent pub to speak of and there was no point in getting a cup of tea, as I knew from my experience of Polish hospitality that I'd be having tea and cake at the old lady's house whether I wanted it or not.

I'd interviewed survivors of trauma before, and I'd had interviewees cry during interviews, but never before I'd even started. I'd always imagined Polish peasants to be a hard breed, taking history's worst cruelties in their stride and not shedding much in the way of tears for themselves, let alone for the plight of an ethnic minority that shared neither their religion nor their cultural traditions. If nothing else, the old lady should provide some good first-hand material for *The History Magazine* – provided she was able to pull herself together and wasn't totally nuts.

After half an hour of sitting in the car, going through my notes and interview questions, I got bored and decided to drive back to the old lady's house and see if she'd talk to me a bit earlier than agreed. This time I knew exactly where I was going, so I was able to concentrate less on houses and house numbers, and more on the road itself. It struck me how deserted it was. Despite having only one lane in each direction, this was the main road heading east from Warsaw, all the way to Belarus; and yet my car seemed to be the only vehicle on it. Not even an old peasant on a hay cart in sight. Perhaps an accident somewhere further up had stopped the traffic, but that would explain the lack of cars in one direction, not both. Perhaps all the other drivers knew something I didn't... I chided myself for letting my imagination run away with me. But as I pulled up alongside the chain-link fence, I couldn't shake the feeling of unease.

The gate was open, as promised. I wondered if I should ring the doorbell anyway, to warn the old lady of my imminent arrival, but I didn't want to bring her all the way out in the cold again, so I slung my bag over my shoulder, locked the car and let myself in, closing the gate behind me. As I headed across the front yard to the rickety old house, a chill breeze stirred around me, whispering in the unmown grass and rustling the leaves of the sapling trees that had seeded themselves and sprouted unchecked on either side of the stone slab path. Although only a dozen or so metres separated me from the old lady's porch, I paused to zip up my parka. As I did so, the breeze grew stronger, making a high-pitched sound as it weaved its way through the eaves of the house. Unexpectedly it died down, and the air around me was as still as the proverbial grave. Then a sudden gust of wind – this time blowing from the direction of the field behind the house. Urgent, angry almost, the wind brought with it something else: a sound – human, yet unearthly; a cry or moan – distant, but so heartfelt and full of despair that, despite the warmth of my down anorak, an icy shiver ran down my spine.

I made my way to the back of the house and looked out over the field that led away to a swampy patch of land, and ended in a stream or river of some sort – obscured by sedges and tall reeds. Beyond the line of water, a wasteland of grass, bushes and wild flowers stretched away to a railway track, and then further, to a dark tree line on the horizon. A mist was rising from the marshy land and, as I peered into the miasma, I thought I saw something: a flash of blue against the grey and brown. The wind blew in my direction again, and this time I was sure that the sound I heard was a young woman weeping.

"Hello!" I called out.

"Hello?" the voice came from behind me, making me jump. "Young man!"

I'd forgotten all about the old lady and my interview. She must have seen me out of a window, and was now holding open the back door, gesticulating for me to come inside. "You'll catch your death of cold!" she chastised gently. I noticed a slight frown crease the woman's already furrowed brow as I threw a last glance back over my shoulder before entering the house. Apart from that passing shadow on her face, my interviewee was a different person from the one I'd left sobbing her heart out almost an hour earlier. Calm and collected, she smiled at me in a warm and friendly manner. When she spoke, her voice was clear and steady.

In no time I found myself sitting in a worn armchair in a small parlour, nursing a glass of black tea in an elaborately engraved silver-coloured holder.

"I'm afraid I don't have much to offer you," said my hostess, holding out a plate with four different types of homemade cake. "You said you wanted to know about the War. I'll tell you everything I remember."

87

Her name was Bronislava. She was born in Międzyrzec and lived with her mother in an apartment block near the town centre. Her street was mixed Polish and Jewish. Not all of the Jews spoke Polish, but most of the Poles spoke at least some Yiddish, and it was normal for children from the two ethnic groups to play together in the street. Bronislava's father had died when she was little and, as her mother was out cleaning for some of the town's more affluent residents during the week, the little girl spent most of her time at the house of her best friends Esther and Mindla, so that her friends' mum was like a second mother to her. Bronislava and Esther were nine when war broke out; Mindla was a couple of years older. For a while not much changed, but slowly, rationing and other increasing restrictions meant that hunger and fear crept into all their lives. Esther and Mindla's family, along with all the other Jewish residents, were ordered to wear armbands with the Star of David, but at this point violence against the Jewish community was incidental rather than systematic.

Then one day, German soldiers with dogs and guns, and auxiliary Ukrainian militia, came marching into Bronislava's street. They swept through the houses, pulling out Jewish families, beating them and leading them away. Bronislava and Esther were playing with the other children. Mindla was out running an errand. When Esther's mother heard all the commotion, she came running out to the two girls, grabbed their hands and tried to pull them away from the shouting soldiers. The three of them were caught and shoved along behind the other Jews. Amid the blows and kicks that rained down on them from all sides, Esther's mother tried to shield the two girls as best she could. Then Bronislava's mother, who had been sewing at home that day, spotted her daughter out of the window across the road, and came running out, shouting that her child was Polish. Somehow she managed to fight her way to Bronislava, and yanked her away from Esther and her mother. Bronislava screamed and grappled with her mother. She tried to go after her best friend, but her mother scooped her up and ran back to their building.

The old woman spoke in a dry, dispassionate, almost robotic way, which I would have found a little disconcerting had I not known that she'd taken some kind of tranquiliser especially for the occasion. She spoke of street roundups, summary executions and coldblooded murder. When she told me about a hyped-up Ukrainian militiaman, in the service of the German military, ripping a baby apart with his bare hands, her voice wavered, and I realised that even with whatever drugs she'd taken, she was making a valiant effort to keep it together.

Some time after Bronislava's Jewish neighbours had been taken away, the German army took over the building in which she and her mother lived, and the remaining residents were evicted. Some of them moved in with extended family elsewhere; others were forcibly re-housed with other Poles.

"We were lucky," Bronislava told me. "My mother had cousins who lived on the outskirts of Międzyrzec – in this very house. Out here things were quieter. The Germans raided the farms to make sure that the peasants weren't hiding any livestock or reserves of grain over the allotted ration quota, but it was easier to grow some vegetables here and occasionally buy a few eggs from a neighbour who'd managed to hang on to a hen or two. My mother and I helped around the house, and my mother still took on the odd cleaning or sewing job, so we got by somehow. We were hungry, but we weren't starving... Would you like some more tea?" I shook my head and she carried on.

"I quickly discovered that there was no love lost between our cousins and the family next door, and the reasons for this became clear soon enough. I know one shouldn't speak ill of the dead," Bronislava frowned, "but there is no other way to speak of those monsters. The farmer was a mean-spirited and violent drunk. His wife was a greedy, spiteful and malicious gossip, and their son, although slimmer in build than his bloated, overfed parents, was a vile combination of the two of them in both temper and habit. As soon as they laid eyes on my mother and me, they hated us with as much venom as they did the rest of our household.

"I asked my aunt how it was that the next-door neighbours were fat and well dressed, while the rest of us were constantly patching up the tatters than hung off our emaciated bodies. And how was it that, when German soldiers carried out their 'inspections', they tore through all the houses – including ours – shouting, kicking things over and showering down blows on anyone who didn't get out of their way fast enough; and yet, when the same soldiers went next door, they joked and chatted with the owner, got drunk with him, and came out clutching food or a bottle of vodka, or sometimes a watch, a piece of jewellery.

"We don't speak about it, my aunt told me. *Just make sure you stay away from them.* Well, being told to stay away from something usually has the opposite effect on little girls, and – despite the horror of those times – I was no different. I spent all my spare time playing in the field at the back of the house and watching the neighbours' property. Then, one evening, my curiosity was rewarded.

"That day, a German patrol had swept through the street, looking for food and valuables. They were in a filthy mood, as nobody had anything left. They trashed our house and hit my uncle across the face when he was unable to give them anything of interest. Finally they went next door and left several hours later, singing and laughing. I figured they wouldn't be back again that evening, so I risked venturing outside.

"The sun had just gone down, but a strange light lingered. It was magic hour, and the field and marshland beyond it glimmered golden-blue. The peculiar light brought out all the blues and purples in the field, so that the cornflowers glowed like luminous azure eyes in the grass. I looked over the tumble-down bit of fence that separated my cousins' land from the neighbours', and my heart skipped a beat. Out in the neighbours' field, a brilliant swathe of bright blue shimmered in the shadows. At first I thought it was mist rising from the damp grass. But it was too solid to be mist and, when it moved, I realised that it was a human figure.

"As quietly as I could, I headed towards it. The figure was small and slim, and I finally worked out that it was a girl – a girl in a blue coat. And then it dawned on me that I'd seen that coat before. The girl turned suddenly, as though sensing my presence. She froze for a moment, then started to run back towards the neighbours' house.

"*Wait!* I clambered over a rotted piece of fence and gave chase. As the girl fled, the hood of her coat came down, and a flurry of matted black tresses flowed out behind her. Despite how thin she now was, I was almost sure. But how could it be? How could someone I'd grieved for every day for three years be alive and fleeing from me through a field that was rapidly turning murky grey?

"The girl was evidently weak, but she had a head start, and I realised I wouldn't catch up with her before she reached the neighbours' house. Desperate, I took a risk and called out. *Mindla? Mindla, wait!* She heard me and stopped dead. She turned towards me slowly, her whole body shaking from the exertion of running barely fifty metres or so. She was emaciated – skeletal almost – no longer the chubby-cheeked twelve-year-old that I'd loved and looked up to, but a gaunt teenager with haunted, hollow eyes. Abruptly magic hour ended, and we were in darkness. We stood facing each other, trembling. Then a small gasp escaped Mindla's cracked lips and, as I rushed towards her, she slumped into my arms.

"From then on, Mindla and I met every night at the border of the two properties in which we were reluctant lodgers. I learned how Mindla had returned from the bakery on that day to find her mother and sister gone. The Polish family next door told her that it wasn't safe for her to stay in the street as the Germans could return at any moment to look for stragglers. She managed to get to the factory where her father worked, but all the Jewish workers had been taken away. So she hid in a series of attics and basements in Międzyrzec, moving on when each hiding-place became unsafe. Finally there was nowhere else to hide, so she left the town one night with a young Jewish woman and her fiancé. They'd tried to survive in the forest, hiding in a hollowed-out tree trunk by day and scavenging for food when it got dark, but when winter started to draw in, the cold and hunger became unbearable. They came across another group of Jews trying to survive in the open, who told them that a Polish peasant was taking in Jewish girls for payment. Mindla knew she wouldn't survive winter in the forest, so she decided to take a chance. She still had a couple of gold coins that her mother had sewn into the lining of her coat when enemy soldiers had first entered the town, so she followed the instructions given and made it to the peasant's house.

"The man told me to give him everything I had, Mindla explained. *In return he would hide me and feed me… But now he says there isn't enough food, so I only get a bowl of soup and a piece of bread a day. During the day I lie hidden behind straw on a kind of shelf above the animals, at the back of the house. That way the Germans don't see me when they come. Sometimes the soldiers stay for hours, drinking homemade vodka with the man and his son. I have to lie very still. I get cramps in my legs, and sometimes bugs crawl on me.*

"Mindla told me about two other Jewish girls who'd been hiding in the peasant's house when she arrived. They'd fled their home village of Rudniki when the 'roundups' started, but the rest of their family had been taken away. One day the peasant and his son came for the sisters in the middle of the night, and Mindla never saw them again. When she asked what had happened to them, the peasant's wife told her to mind her own business, and the peasant said that a relative of theirs had come and taken them away. But Mindla must have had doubts as to the girls' plight because she kept returning to them in our conversations.

"I told Mindla that I would ask my mother if she could stay with us. *No,* said Mindla. *I won't put your lives in danger.* I related our conversation to my mother, and she said that Mindla was right; we didn't have the privileges that the next-door neighbour had – unlike his house, ours got searched from top to bottom – and, in any case, there were no hiding-places in our house. So Mindla and I met outdoors, sometimes in the pouring rain. I lived for those meetings. I put aside what little food I could, as did my mother. We didn't tell my cousins what I was up to. The fewer who knew, the better. Sometimes my mother caught me sneaking out at night. She was very afraid for me, but she didn't stop me.

"One night Mindla was late to meet me. Finally she appeared, looking paler and more frightened than normal. She usually managed a wan smile and a few words when she saw me, but this time she was withdrawn and silent. It took me a while to get her to admit what had happened. The farmer had become tired of hiding her and feeding her. He said that he wanted payment. *I said that I'd already given him everything, and he said 'Not everything.'* Mindla cried as she told me that the man had tried to force himself on her. She was only saved because her screams brought out the man's wife, who called her 'an ungrateful little whore', and dragged her husband back to bed. I don't think I fully comprehended what Mindla was telling me – at twelve I was very naive about the ways of the world – but I knew that my beloved friend was in trouble and that I had to do something. *Let's run away together*, I told her. *Let's go right now – tonight.* Mindla looked at me with love and sadness. I've never seen such sadness in anybody's eyes. *We can't run away*, she told me. *There's nowhere to run.*

"That night I had a terrible nightmare. Mindla was standing by the marsh at the bottom of the field. She was only in her underwear. She reached out to me and at first I thought that she had that same sadness in her eyes, but as I drew closer, I saw that her eyes were gone." Bronislava paused. I had been engrossed in her recollection, and the sudden silence startled me. I looked at her, but she avoided my gaze. She turned away and pretended to blow her nose, but I could see that she was wiping her eyes.

"The next night Mindla didn't come," she finally said, then fell silent once more. I waited in vain for her to speak. After what seemed like a long time, but was probably only half a minute, I finally asked her what had happened.

"I waited for hours," she said. It was raining and very cold. Eventually my mother came out and found me by the fence, soaking wet. I contracted pneumonia and nearly died." Another pause.

"What happened to Mindla?"

"She was never seen again."

"Well, what do you think happened to her?"

"I don't *think*. I *know* what happened. They killed her. The farmer and that son of his. As soon as I saw my Mindla's blue coat stretched over the grotesque body of that woman, I knew that they'd killed her."

"You saw the farmer's wife wearing Mindla's coat?"

"Yes. When I was well enough to get out of bed, I looked out of the window and saw her parading around shamelessly in it. It had always been too big for Mindla. I remember, she'd seen that coat in a shop and fallen in love with it. That was just before war broke out. She persuaded her mother that she'd 'grow into it' and eventually her mother gave in and bought it for her. But Mindla never grew into it. Instead of filling out like other girls her age, she'd been starved and the coat always hung off her. But it was too small for that awful woman – she couldn't even do the buttons up, and yet she strutted around in it as though Mindla had never existed. God knows why she wanted it – it was tattered and badly worn, but it was a pretty colour, and the woman was greedy.

"I flew out of the house before my aunt could stop me, and I confronted her. I asked what she'd done to Mindla. The woman shouted at me to mind my own business. Her husband came storming out of the house and told me that if I didn't shut up, he'd make sure that something very bad happened to me.

"The next thing I knew, German soldiers came storming into my cousins' house. They beat up my uncle and tore up the floorboards in the kitchen. The next-door neighbour had told them that we'd hidden grain under the floor. They didn't find anything, and the farmer got a clout round the ear hole for making them waste their time, but he'd made his point.

"I didn't confront him again until the war was over. The communist authorities weren't interested in the wild accusations of an adolescent girl – or her mother. In any case, the farmer was a man of influence. He had grown wealthy on the suffering of the unfortunate souls he had exploited and, although the other residents on the street viewed him with distaste and went out of

their way to avoid him, he didn't care. He now drank with the
NKVD, and, when the Soviets left Poland to the Polish
communists, he drank with the chief of police. It was made very
clear to me that if I continued with my accusations, things would
end very badly for my mother. By the time the communists were
overthrown, the farmer and his family were dead. The man and
his wife died of natural causes, but not until they had buried their
only son. It's said that he was drunk and – for some inexplicable
reason – wandered out onto the tracks beyond the field at the
back of his parents' house, where he was hit by a train." The old
lady paused, and I thought that she'd finished her story. I tried to
think of something appropriate to say, but after a moment's
hesitation, during which she seemed to be sizing me up, she
carried on.

"Sometimes I dream about her," she said. "Sometimes,
especially in autumn and in early spring, when the mist rises
from the marshy ground, I see her walking along the ditch at the
far end of the field. Mostly I just hear her crying…" The woman
broke off, tired and sad. I could tell I wasn't going to get much
more out of her. She fixed her rheumy eyes on me, and seemed
to wait for my full attention. I placed my glass of tea carefully on
the table and returned her gaze. Something in her tone changed;
became more urgent, almost pleading. "I've waited fifty years to
tell her story to someone who would listen," she finally said. "To
someone who could tell her story to the world and … right the
wrong."

I lowered my eyes and finished my honey cake, weighing up
whether or not to tell my down-to-earth editor the story of the
girl in the blue coat. As I sipped the last of my tea, I already
knew that the 'ghost story' wouldn't make it into my research
notes…I know what you're thinking, but, in any case, it wouldn't
have made a difference; my boss dropped the Międzyrzec story.
It wasn't that he was unhappy with my report – quite the
contrary; I'd managed to find two credible eyewitnesses of the
so-called 'ghetto liquidations', during which the Jews who had
been rounded up or enticed out of hiding with promises of
immunity were robbed, beaten and murdered, or herded onto

trucks and driven to the local train station for transportation to the gas chambers of Treblinka and Majdanek... No, my research had been thorough, as ever, but the ghetto liquidation story was abandoned in favour of the Chelmno death camp; aerial photography had uncovered a hitherto unknown mass grave in the nearby forest, and my boss was keen for *The History Magazine* to be the first publication outside Poland to cover the find.

And so I forgot all about Międzyrzec, and the old lady, and the girl in the blue coat. Until fifteen years later – when I was working as a war correspondent for Reuters in war-torn Iraq. I'd been stationed with the US regiment I told you about for over a month. We'd been lucky: the territory that came under our patrols was fairly quiet, and the worst thing about the posting was the heat and the desert wind. No matter how carefully you covered up, you could always taste sand in your mouth, and the grit would irritate your nose and make your eyes run – despite the shades we all wore virtually around the clock.

Then one night I saw her – the dead girl from Międzyrzec. She stood in the mist at the bottom of the old woman's field, looking at me with eyes of death and sorrow. The cold blue-grey of that Polish landscape couldn't have been further from the blistering yellow of the desert into which I awoke, and yet no amount of burning desert dust could dispel the horror I felt. That day the convoy I was travelling with drove into a trap – a double whammy, if you like – of a landmine and a car-bomb driven by a suicide bomber, who died on the spot, along with five of the soldiers who'd become my friends over the past few weeks. Nobody escaped without injury; some of us lost limbs, one young man from Idaho lost an eye, another boy lost part of his jaw. I was lucky; I escaped with shrapnel in my knee and cuts to my back and arms. But it shook my confidence in my indestructibility – for a while, at least.

With all the blood and guts and horror of the aftermath of the attack, I forgot about the girl in the blue coat once more. But she came back. Whenever I became complacent, whenever things were going a bit too well, or when I simply forgot about my own mortality, she came back. Don't get me wrong, people weren't blown up around me every time I dreamt about her, but each time reminded me of the unpredictability and cruelty of the world we live in; of death which will one day come for all of us, and of the fact that she's still waiting – waiting out there in the cold, the damp and the dark for her story to be told... And I've been dreaming a lot lately.

I see I've rendered you speechless. Well, I'm sorry. Like the old lady in Międzyrzec, I've waited many years to tell that story. I realise it doesn't quite fit with the image of the tough old reporter that we've created together, but you must promise to allow me to tell it to the world as I've told it to you today. You know it now. And, believe me, if either of us is to have any peace in this world or the next, then it must be told. Promise me.

"His words, not mine," the ghostwriter looked his publisher straight in the eye. "So you see, we have to keep it in. It's what he wanted." It was a plea more than a statement.

"Nonsense!" the publisher scoffed. The writer's sentimentality and inexperience were starting to annoy him. Perhaps it had been a mistake to give the Johnson gig to someone so young. "Don't you see? A supernatural yarn about a dead girl goes against everything else you've written. It's out of character, it's completely inconsistent with the rest of the book; it will alienate our readers and ruin Johnson's reputation."

"You don't understand ..." the writer implored.

"But I do understand. I understand that including a drugged-up old man's fantasies in what is to be his legacy to the world would not just be *unfair* to Frank; it would be a total violation of the trust he placed in all of us to tell his story." The publisher studied the writer closely. The young man's face had blanched and he was starting to sweat. "Look," the older man's voice softened a little, "Frank Johnson was hard as nails. Not a fanciful bone in his body. If he'd been in his right mind the last time you saw him, he'd never have said what he said. He was a tough, unshakeable war correspondent who did a dangerous and responsible job, and did it well – you know that better than anyone. Now his reputation is in our hands. And there's no way this publishing house is going to destroy his legacy for the sake of some crazy story that he told you in his last days, high on morphine."

The writer had lowered his gaze to his hands, which were clasping and unclasping in his lap like the death throes of a beached fish. When he raised his eyes again, the publisher was shocked to see in them a look of desperation and – perhaps – fear. When he finally spoke, his voice shook, and for a moment the publisher had the worrying notion that the writer was going to burst into tears.

"You don't understand," the young man practically begged. "I've ... seen her."

"What? ... Who?"

"The girl." The publisher stared at the writer uncomprehendingly. "The girl in the blue coat."

"What do you mean? Where?" The publisher wasn't sure what disturbed him more: the writer's evident breakdown or the fact that he now found himself alone in a room with a madman.

"In my dreams... Nightmares." The writer looked down at his now motionless hands. "She walks along the ditch at the bottom of a field. It's cold. It's lonely. When the wind blows in my direction, I can hear her crying. And then she looks at me... I see her every night... Her eyes are like death. Full of betrayal and sorrow that can never be healed. Grief not just for her own short, painful existence, but for all those whose bones or ashes lie in unmarked graves. I can't stand her eyes. The desolation in them gets inside you. It makes you wish you were dead. Makes you wish you'd never been born..." The publisher was too stunned to react and, after a moment's pause, the writer carried on. "I don't know how Frank Johnson lived with it... He was a ... strong ... man." The writer raised his eyes once more, but did not meet his boss's incredulous gaze. His attention was focused on the window at the far end of the office, behind his listener's back, where something – a gust from the air-conditioning unit perhaps – caused the reinforced textile strips of the cream-coloured blind

to stir and rattle softly against the glass pane. He added quietly,
"I'm not ... that ... strong ..."

A TALE OF TWO SISTERS
I
RUSALKA

Full fathom five thy father lies;
Of his bones are coral made;
Those are pearls that were his eyes:
Nothing of him that doth fade,
But doth suffer a sea-change
Into something rich and strange.

— William Shakespeare, *The Tempest*

A Tale of Two Sisters: Rusalka

I always loved Shakespeare at school. Never went on to college. I guess the possibility just didn't figure on anybody's radar. Once I turned sixteen and school was over, I went straight back to work on my parents' farm. But I didn't stop reading. The number of times my father caught me stretched out under the oak tree at the far end of the north field with a copy of Macbeth or King Lear... Once, in a fit of rage, he swore he'd cut the old tree down, and he did too. But don't think that my father was a bad man – not at all. He just worried that he would die and leave my mother with no one to take care of her. He loved my mother, you see – loved her like a man possessed. He wouldn't let her sew at night lest she strain her eyes; he wouldn't let her help in the fields so she wouldn't become all hunched over and sore-backed like the other women in the village. He wouldn't even let her milk the cow in case she got cowpox and her dainty little hands grew blistered and calloused. Very delicate she was – my mother. Pale-skinned and raven-haired, with haunted green eyes. My father always said that she'd married beneath her, and that he was the luckiest man in the world.

But my father shouldn't have worried; it was my mother who died first. Cancer, the doctors said. Her cheeks grew gaunt and her whole face appeared to recede until her huge frightened eyes seemed to be all that was left, like a pair of emerald moons shining brightest before their eclipse. Her slender body shrivelled away to nothing. And her raven locks became streaked with white, then fell from her scalp after the hospital treatment – like discarded angel-hair once the festive season is over and Christmas trees are thrown on the compost heap to rot. My father's cries were pitiful to hear. His violent episodes became more frequent as his drinking increased; my mother – the only thing that had stood between him and his baser nature – was gone. He didn't hit me – as even through the veil of cheap whiskey he must have remembered my mother's screams the one time he'd laid a hand on me – but he found my books and burned them. *Coriolanus, Hamlet, As You Like It*, all the tattered copies of the Histories and Tragedies I had acquired from second-hand bookstores in the nearest town with the pennies my mother had slipped me out of her housekeeping money. All gone up in smoke. Only *The Tempest* escaped annihilation. I think my father simply hadn't seen it – for there is no other explanation as to its survival. It was as if Prospero had come out of retirement and conjured up a supernatural mist – shrouding the small volume and rendering it invisible for five long minutes while my father rampaged through my tiny room. Or some such thing. When my father finally fell asleep on the kitchen table, tears in his eyes and an empty bottle in his hand, I picked up *The Tempest* and left. I never saw my father again.

Four years later, aged twenty-two now and having worked my way across Europe doing odd jobs, I found myself in Eastern Poland. I'd wanted to come here for some time, as my mother had mentioned that her mother came from a village in this part of the world. I hadn't pushed her on the subject, as it always seemed to make her sad; I gather that the family had fled some pogrom or other when the Russians occupied the region. But I regretted not having asked exactly which village it was…

The country was beginning to recover from forty-five years of communism, but nobody had told the peasants in its easternmost areas. Here people still scratched a meagre living from the difficult soil.

I'd saved some money working as a hotel receptionist in Lublin, and I knocked around the countryside, half-heartedly looking for my grandmother's village, and whole-heartedly enjoying the exotic landscape of ramshackle settlements and unspoilt forests.

I fell in love with the little village of Switeziec at once, and took up temporary residence with an old lady who let rooms and cooked a great breakfast. To my delight, her grandson Piotr – a friendly young man of eighteen or so – knew a little English; and what he didn't know, he made up for in enthusiasm, expansive gestures and an easy laugh, which always seemed to be bubbling just under the surface, ready to erupt.

"They start to teach English in school as soon as compulsory Russian was kicked out," laughed Piotr when I expressed my surprise at his linguistic skills. I couldn't help but think that Piotr made a nice change from the serious, somewhat gloomy majority of young Polish men I'd come across so far. Young men who reminded me too much of ... well ... me. Yes, I realised that laughter was something that didn't come easily to me, and I often chided myself for my inability to kick back and have fun.

"You come to Switeziec at good time," Piotr flashed a full set of healthy-looking teeth at me. "We have big party tonight." I waited for Piotr to continue, then realised that he was awaiting my response.

"Oh, I see. Well. Thanks for mentioning it, Piotr, but I've got to get an early start tomorrow if I'm going to get to the next village..." Piotr blinked uncomprehendingly. "You remember what we spoke about? – I'm trying to find the village my grandmother's family came from?"

"Oh, I see." Piotr looked crestfallen for a moment, but the teeth were out again soon enough. "But tonight is very special night. It's ... longest day. Very special."

"Oh. Midsummer's Eve? ... So it is."

"Yes. We have very special party. It's tradition. We have fire and the girls make ... out of flowers ... and light candles ... and put them on river, and the boys have to catch them."

"What?"

"I not explain well..." Piotr's frustration was painful to watch. "It's tradition... You will like... Please, you come with me." Whether it was a chance to practise his English, or to show off his foreign friend to the other villagers, or just his innate friendliness and desire to be a great host that rendered my presence so seemingly important to him, I don't know, but when Piotr's smile started to waver, I gave in. So, later that evening I found myself following him and a group of his friends to the river that flowed west of the village.

Twilight had been slow in coming. Beyond the various shades of grey, an orange glow emanated from the riverbank. As we got closer, the sounds of singing and laughter steadily grew. There was a large bonfire on the nearside. Young men sat around,

103

drinking beers and talking excitedly. On the far bank, and about fifty metres upriver, was another bonfire.

"The girls are making … erm … out of flowers," Piotr tried to explain, following my gaze. "Like this." He used both hands to draw a circle in the air.

"Wreaths?" I suggested.

"Yes, wreaths… Normally you put on head, like this," Piotr demonstrated by lifting the invisible circle and placing it on his head, "but today they put candles in them and put them on river." I nodded, doing my best to understand.

"The boys catch the … wreaths. And when a boy catch the wreath, he can kiss the girl who made it."

"I see… But how do you know whose wreath you've fished out?"

"Oh, I think the boys – they just kiss the girl they like."

"That sounds like cheating to me," I quipped.

Piotr looked at me, worked out that I was joking, and started to laugh.

There was a flurry of giggling and excited shrieks from the far side of the river.

"Look!" cried Piotr, "Girls put wreaths on water!" And sure enough, a dozen or so little lights came floating in our direction. Some went out almost immediately, others sank without a trace, but a few continued to float and burn, carried downriver by the strong current.

Piotr's friends giggled no less than the girls, and rushed down the bank with the other youths.

"Come on!" Piotr called out as he hurried after the others, who were already braving the freezing water to intercept those wreaths that hadn't yet drowned.

I followed cautiously, afraid of slipping and falling in. I'd always been scared of water; even before the time when my father had tried to teach me to swim. He'd used the same method his father had used on him: he'd rowed us out to the middle of the lake near our farm, and pushed me out of the boat. I don't remember much after that, except that he'd had to fish me out himself; his anger at having to get wet tempered by the fear that he'd actually drowned me and that the shock would kill my mother. He never gave me another swimming lesson, evidently deciding that having a pathetic runt of a son was better than having a dead one.

The mirth on the riverbank was infectious, and I couldn't help but smile as Piotr beat his friend to a wreath and pulled it out of the water, waving it in the air and whooping in triumph. Then I saw something that stopped the breath in my lungs.

She was standing between the willows on the far bank, a little aside from the other girls. The light from the bonfire seemed to die before it reached her, and she was bathed in shadow. At first I thought that one of the willows had moved, and I felt startled and disorientated. As I peered into the gloom, my eyes adjusted, and then I saw her quite plainly ... no, 'plainly' is the wrong word – for there was nothing plain about her at all. The bonfire, the singing, the shouts and laughter – everything subsided and disappeared for a moment. All I was aware of was the girl on the other side of the river. She was tall and slender, her dress as pale as her delicate features. Her waist-long hair was so fair it seemed to glow blue in the twilight. As I stared, the girl turned to face me, and I finally understood what people meant when they said that their heart had skipped a beat. I paused, steadying myself, and inhaled deeply. She smiled at me and, despite the distance and the scant light, I could tell that her lips were the colour of coral. Every detail of her form was etched into my memory from that moment on, forever. The only strange thing was – perhaps because she tilted her head down shyly, perhaps because a strand of flaxen hair fell across her face – I couldn't see her eyes.

The girl waved at me; her hand small, with long, tapering fingers. I looked around to see whether she could be waving at someone else, but there was no one behind or next to me. Hesitantly, I waved back, and she waved again, beckoning me to join her on the far bank. My heart beat so fast I could hardly breathe.

"Piotr!" I ran up to the boy and grabbed his arm.

"Hey," he turned towards me and grinned. "Look! I have a wreath."

"Where can I cross the river?"

"Huh?"

"Where's the nearest place I can cross the river?" I slowed my words right down, articulating each one as clearly as I could.

"Just there, to the right," Piotr's confusion was replaced by mere surprise, and he pointed downriver. I peered into the darkness, but saw nothing. "There are logs put on river. About twenty metres that way," continued Piotr, adding, "Hey, why do you want to go to girls' side anyway?" Then he grinned, "It's cheating!"

"The girl," was all I managed by way of an explanation.

"It's cheating," Piotr repeated, laughing. "You're supposed to catch a wreath first... Anyway, which girl it is you like?"

"The girl," I pointed across the water, but she was gone. An indescribable, overwhelming feeling of loss and longing came over me; I felt like I'd been kicked in the stomach and I figured I must be having a panic attack of some sort.

"What girl?" laughed Piotr, then stopped laughing as he saw the look on my face.

"The blonde girl," I tried to explain, my eyes scouring the opposite bank. "Look, Piotr, thanks," I stammered. "I've got to go."

I staggered off in the direction of the makeshift bridge, leaving a perplexed Piotr muttering to his friends – something about the lovelorn foreigner, no doubt.

Soon I was standing next to the bridge – a couple of logs thrown over the fast-flowing river. I stared down into the murky water.

Full fathom five thy father lies.

If I had any chance at all of finding the girl, I'd have to get a move on. I placed my right foot on one of the logs, then, checking to make sure there was nobody watching, I got down on my hands and knees, tested the logs and started to crawl along them, one hand and knee on one log, one on the other.

The gushing noise of the current made me feel giddy. I determined to crawl straight over to the other side, without

looking down. I made it about halfway across, but then I caught
sight of something white in the water to my left.

Of his bones are coral made.

I came to an unsteady halt. I could hear my breath coming in
short gasps and my heart beating – a blessing, I thought, as it
seemed to drown out the hideous hiss of the river. Holding onto
the rough bark of the logs, I glanced down to my left.

Nothing: only blackness and the rushing, hissing water. I took
a deep breath and moved off slowly. It came again: a silvery
flash in the water, caught out of the corner of my eye.

I jerked my head in the direction of whatever it was, digging
my fingers into the wood and flattening myself against the logs
for fear of falling in. And I saw it: a pale shape floating just
beneath the surface of the inky water. In my fear, I thought I
could make out a human face, and for a moment I believed I was
looking at a corpse.

Those are pearls that were his eyes.

But then the thing disappeared upriver, apparently swimming
against the strong current. Once I stopped trembling, I crawled as
quickly as I dared to the far side. I stood up shakily and looked
upriver. Nothing there. As my heartbeat returned to normal, I
told myself that I'd imagined everything; that my innate fear of
death by water had conjured up visions of corpse-like monsters
to torment me.

Then I remembered the girl, and that unbearable feeling of
sadness and yearning returned. I hurried up the bank, unnerved
by the willows, which looked like frozen human forms in the
half-light, and headed upriver.

As I approached the girls' bonfire, I looked in vain for the girl
with the flaxen hair. The other girls didn't notice me at first, but
as my search grew more desperate, a couple of them spotted me.
They approached, giggling, and searched me for any sign of a
wreath, telling me off and shooing me away amicably when they
found no sign of one. I stumbled past the bonfire and into the
forest beyond.

The forest was a frightening place at night. The darkness was full of noises – rustling and scuttling, as startled animals fled before me into the undergrowth. Never for a moment did I stop to think about what I was doing. I only knew that if I didn't find the girl, my heart would break – indeed, it was breaking already.

"Hello?" I called out, peering between the ancient trees. "Are you there?" Only the wind answered, sighing in the branches. For a moment I thought I glimpsed something white flitting in between the trees nearest the river. "Hey!" I called out, and tried to run, but tripped on a root and almost fell. I righted myself by grabbing hold of a tree, scratching my hand painfully in the process. When I looked up again, there was nothing between the trees, but shadow. I stumbled on in this inept and idiotic way, imagining from time to time that I could see a wisp of blue-white hair ahead of me, stopping only when the dawn chorus broke through my desperate reveries and a rosy glimmer appeared in the east. Defeated and exhausted, I turned around and headed back along the river.

The shouts and laughter, and glow of the bonfire reached me before I broke clear of the tree line. I was surprised to find the young villagers still partying. The boys and girls had largely paired off, and were holding hands and leaping across the fairly feisty remains of the fire. Had I been in a fit state to appreciate what was going on around me, I would no doubt have concluded that their stamina and party spirit was something to be admired, even if the local vodka was a contributing factor.

"Hey!" someone called, and then Piotr was patting me on the back and laughing – a relieved kind of laugh. "Where have you been? I been worried for you!"

"I'm sorry, Piotr," I muttered gloomily.

"Where you were?"

"I was looking for the girl," I told him, but didn't expect to make him understand.

"What girl? All the girls are here..." I must have looked as shattered and distressed as I was feeling, because Piotr put his arm around my shoulders and said, "Come on, my friend, we go home." I protested weakly, mumbling something about having to look for the girl. "Come on, man," Piotr steered me in a friendly, but firm manner away from the river. "You look terrible. You need sleep."

"But…"

"I help you look for girl tomorrow … or actually, later today." Piotr winked at a cute redheaded girl and whispered something to her that made her smile, then led me back to his grandmother's house.

I fell into an exhausted sleep – punctuated by dreams of floating corpses, dark forests, and the girl disappearing among the trees – and woke at lunchtime. I got dressed and sloped downstairs, presumably looking awful, as a worried look appeared on Piotr's grandmother's face when she saw me. She asked Piotr a question and he shrugged her off, in a not unfriendly manner. He pushed an empty chair away from the table, inviting me to sit down. I forced myself to sit, but every nerve in my body was crying out to get back outside and look for the girl.

Piotr's grandmother busied herself at the stove, and moments later set a bowl of hot hunter's stew down in front of me, along with a small basket of fresh rye bread. I hadn't eaten since the previous evening and yet, when Piotr's grandmother gestured for me to eat, I found that I couldn't.

"I'm sorry," I said, feeling miserable and ungrateful.

"You feel bad?" asked Piotr, the concern in his face echoing that in his grandmother's.

"The girl," I said. "I have to find her." I rose swiftly, apologised again to Piotr's grandmother, and headed for the door.

"Wait!" Piotr got up and ran after me. "I come with you!"

A couple of hours later, Piotr persuaded me to return to the house for fear that I would pass out. Reluctantly I succumbed, drinking a cup of sweet tea and packing a chunk of bread, before heading back out, much to the chagrin of Piotr's grandmother.

"I come with you," said Piotr, somewhat less enthusiastically than earlier.

"No," I insisted. "You stay here; your grandmother looks worried." I left quickly, hearing Piotr and his grandmother arguing as I walked away.

I spent the rest of the day following the Swita River first one way, then the other. Once or twice I thought I saw something pale shimmering in the water, but when I turned to look, it was gone. When my feet grew too sore to keep walking, I returned to the house and tried to sleep. I tossed and turned, and attempted to free my mind of thoughts, but whenever I closed my eyes, I saw the girl waving to me from the row of willows. The terrible yearning and hopelessness gnawed away at me, and I'm ashamed to say that I cried into my pillow. I finally dozed off a little before dawn, and got up late again.

As I entered the kitchen, Piotr's grandmother eyed me with unease.

"*Piotrusiu!*" she called, and a moment later Piotr appeared, smiling at me in a worried way that I was coming to dislike. There was a brief exchange between the two of them, during which the look on the old woman's face became progressively more alarmed. She said something to Piotr, who laughed, causing her to brandish a wooden spoon at him in a less than friendly gesture. She cast me an extremely troubled glance, then returned her attention to the frying pan.

"Are you okay?" asked Piotr.

"I'm fine," I said, forcing myself to smile at the old lady as she set a plate of ham and eggs down in front of me before sitting down opposite and staring at me intently.

"What you are going to do today?" questioned Piotr with feigned cheerfulness; then added doubtfully, "You are going to look for your grandmother's village?"

"No."

"You are going to look for girl?"

"Yes."

Piotr's grandmother evidently asked Piotr what I'd said. The boy translated, and the old lady leapt up from the table, glanced at me, then let out a tirade at her grandson, who was looking more and more embarrassed.

"What did she say?" I asked.

"Nothing," said Piotr.

"Tell me, please."

"It's rubbish. Stupid story."

"Piotr!" I pleaded, and the old lady interjected on my behalf.

"Okay," Piotr finally gave in. "My grandmother says your girl is Rusalka."

"Who?"

"Rusalka. A bad spirit."

"What do you mean?"

"It's an old story that the peasants tell."

"Go on."

"They say that if a girl dies ... violent death, or kill herself ... she becomes Rusalka. A bad spirit. They live in water and in trees."

"Like nymphs?" If I hadn't been in such a sorry state, I probably would have found Piotr's story entertaining.

"Yes... Stupid story."

"Yes," I agreed. Then I noticed Piotr's grandmother still staring at me and nodding her head gravely. "But please tell your grandmother not to worry. The girl I saw isn't a... Rusalka. She's a girl, and I'm worried that something might have happened to her. I need to find her." I got up and headed out, stopping Piotr from following me with a staying hand gesture.

The day passed much as the previous one, except that the sadness and feeling I can only describe as emptiness was even stronger than before. It was as though I'd lost a limb, but could still feel intense pain where it had once been.

I went home when it got dark, and went to bed without speaking to Piotr. I couldn't face his questions or his grandmother's look of concern. I lay awake for a long time, looking at the ceiling. When I finally closed my eyes, the full moon rose outside my window, its light unnerving me even through closed lids. I could swear I heard someone whispering my name, and I turned to the window. The moonlight was silver-blue, like the girl's hair. The whispering came again and the sighing of the wind in the branches of the tree outside.

111

Eventually I could lie there no longer. I got dressed, crept as quietly as I could along the creaky wooden floor, and headed for the river.

The fields were a pale grey, and beyond them the river sparkled silver. I planned to start at the makeshift bridge, then work my way upriver and into the forest. I walked along distractedly and didn't notice that I was approaching the water a little upriver of my chosen starting point. In fact, it wasn't until I was at the river's edge that I noticed I'd come out amidst the willows – in almost the same place as I'd seen the girl. Startled out of my stupor by that thought, I looked across to where she'd stood. I thought I heard my name whispered on the wind, and then I saw a willow move in the pale light. No, not a willow – her! Standing on the opposite side of the river, now as she had the first time I'd seen her, but even more beautiful in the moonlight, even more heart-stopping. A shiver ran down my spine and goose bumps appeared on my skin despite the warm June night. The girl's hair was so pale that it glowed blue in the moon's rays, and her lips were the colour of coral. I tried, but I couldn't see her eyes. She smiled at me and waved, beckoning me to join her on the other side of the river. Mesmerised, I took a step forward, then stopped as my foot slipped on the soft mud of the riverbank and I nearly lost my footing. I looked down at the rushing, roaring current and felt dizzy. But I had to get to her somehow.

"Wait!" I pleaded. "I'll cross over the bridge!" But she was already moving off in the opposite direction. "Wait, please!" I ran a few steps towards the bridge, then turned quickly and ran after the girl, keeping track of her across the river as she moved in and out of the willows, smiling and waving to me. Each time her slim form disappeared from my field of vision, it was like a stab to my heart. I'd missed my opportunity to cross the bridge to her side of the river, but I wouldn't let her out of my sight for more than a split-second.

"Hey, slow down! Please!" I followed her upriver. The solitary willows gave way to clusters of birch, oak and pine, and soon we were in the forest, the river between us all the while. She was the

112

most beautiful thing one could imagine; she was a silvery-blue angel, shining among the dark monoliths of the trees. I panicked as she disappeared from view, and quickened my pace.

"Where are you?" I practically begged, hurrying deeper and deeper into the forest. "Please! Where are you?" Light-headed with anxiety, I stopped and peered across the river. For a moment all was still and I was alone with my own heartbeat once again. A stab of fear and that overpowering sense of loss assaulted me for a moment, and then I saw her. She moved from behind a tree and stood directly opposite me on the far side of the river. Naked. The moonlight reflected off her lily-white skin and blue-blonde hair. Her body was perfection, and she stood quite still, gazing at me, frozen like the alabaster statue of a goddess. I heard my name whispered in the air, and the girl moved so gracefully that she seemed to float down to the water's edge. She waved to me, beckoning me to approach the river on my side. I got as close to the water as I dared, then stopped and watched the girl go in.

"No!" I called out in alarm. "Don't." But the girl merely laughed and immersed herself in the river, the water covering her nakedness. She waved to me to join her, and I waved back, pleading with her to come to my side. The girl laughed and swam over to my side, then swam leisurely back to the middle of the river and floated there. The ease with which she swam and floated in that rushing water made me wonder whether perhaps the current was less strong that it looked and sounded. Perhaps the water wasn't as deep as I'd thought.

The girl beckoned me again and I shook my head, indicating for her to swim to me and come out. I held a hand out to her, and eventually she swam towards me, stopping just a little out of my reach. I extended my hand out further, and she pushed herself up from the water and reached out to me. As she did so, the drops of water on her breasts sparkled like diamonds. I couldn't take my eyes off her. She moved away again and I lost my balance, toppling into the icy water.

Fear – all the more dreadful for its long-forgotten familiarity – seized me as the dark waters closed over my head. I flailed my arms wildly, managing somehow to right myself and get my head above the surface. Eyes screwed shut against the lashing current, I coughed up water and finally managed to scream for help. Then I felt arms around me – arms colder than the river against which I fought.

"Help me," I begged through the roar of the raging water – water that no longer looked silver, but black and threatening. I felt the brush of wet hair on my face and of icy lips against my ear – lips colder than the spray that blinded me. The girl whispered my name, and her voice was the sigh of the wind and the murmur of the sea. For a moment I remembered my mother and how she would hold a large shell to my ear when I was little, and say, "Listen, my love, it's the sound of the sea."

The girl's grip on me tightened and I prayed that she would save me, but the water closed over my head once more.

I try to draw breath, but swallow river-water instead. I don't understand. I kick and writhe, but cold hands pull me down and hold me firm.

Gradually I weaken and stop fighting. My terror subsides and I open my eyes. In the blackness, the girl's face looms white before my own. She lifts her heavy lids and I see her eyes clearly for the first time. Fear seizes me once more; the last of my air escapes in a flurry of bubbles as I panic. She holds onto me and smiles, gazing at me with those eyes – a corpse's eyes: milky, opaque ... like pearls.

My lungs swell with water. A strange calm descends on me and I stop struggling for the last time. The girl cradles me in her arms.

I wonder if the current will carry me down to the sea...

II
FIRST NIGHT

They chased the fleeing girl relentlessly, their horses snorting and sweating in the sultry air. Sooner or later they would catch her – she knew that, and headed for the lake at the edge of the village. For a while she lost her pursuers among the dense trees. A fresh wave of tears stained her youthful face as she burst out onto the bank. There she paused a moment, trying to catch her breath amidst the beauty of the desolate place with its vast expanse of dark water and row of weeping willows, their leaves rustling uneasily as she moved past them towards the water's edge. She could hear the shouts and the thunder of hooves coming closer. Dizzy with fear and exhaustion, she leaned for a moment against a willow tree. Then, casting a final glance over her shoulder, she threw herself forward. In that final second, her thoughts turned to her beloved. Her heart was broken even before the dark waters closed over her head.

The willow trailed its leaves in the water like verdant tears. Its branches stirred restlessly as the horse and cart struggled past, headed for the village guesthouse.

"Splendid!" remarked Henry, looking in the direction of the lake. Dan followed his gaze, expecting to spy some new marvel amidst the stunning rural landscape, but instead saw two local girls, one with long brown her plaited down her back and the other wearing a traditional flowery headscarf. Henry waved at them, and they waved back, giggling. He turned back to his companion. "I think we're in there, old man," he informed Dan with a grin.

"Right," Dan was unconvinced. Then again, the ladies seemed to go for Henry's ex-public schoolboy charms and, the two of them being exotic foreigners, even Dan was getting a bit of female attention.

"Aren't you glad we didn't take a cab after all!" It was a statement rather than a question, but Dan felt that a response was expected nonetheless.

"Right," he agreed uncertainly and tightened his grip on the side of the cart, his eyes glued to the peasant's back and the horse's rump beyond. Dan came from a stalwart middle class family in Birmingham, and horses were not something he'd ever planned on getting this close to. But Henry was evidently loving the whole Eastern European thing. Dan couldn't help but wonder how strange it was that Henry of all people – Henry who, despite his foreign surname, was to all intents and purposes more English than the Queen – should go haring around Poland, looking for traces of his ancestors. Still and all, perhaps it was less un-PC than exploring the colonialist past on his mother's side. In any case, Dan enjoyed Henry's company and was happy to tag along.

Eventually the road led away from the lake and uphill a little. The horse snorted and strained onwards, foamy sweat dripping from its sides. Dan sighed with relief as the cart rolled to a halt outside the quaint old building that served as the local guesthouse.

"Good evening," the receptionist smiled at Henry in a manner that Dan was beginning to find a little annoying.

Several hours and a considerable number of vodkas later, Dan turned up the Polish sitcom on his TV in a vain attempt to drown out the sounds of Henry entertaining the receptionist in the room next door. Henry and Dan had dined together, then sat at the hotel bar, where the receptionist doubled as barmaid. The two Brits seemed to be the only visitors at the small guesthouse, and Henry had taken advantage of the lack of other customers to persuade the Polish girl to join them in a few drinks. Eventually Dan had made his excuses and gone up to his room, leaving Henry and the girl to their own devices. It hadn't been long, however, before he'd heard them entering Henry's room.

Dan flicked through the channels, trying to find something he could actually watch, but even the American blockbusters had a lector reading the Polish translation over the English dialogue in a way that rendered both languages less than audible. He turned off the TV. The moaning, creaking bedsprings and banging of Henry's bed against the wall stopped temporarily, and Dan became aware of the wind sighing outside his window. He opened it wide and leaned out. From his vantage point on the top floor he could see the lake along which they had travelled on their way to the hotel. From what Dan had worked out, it formed part of an extensive complex of lakes and waterways, stretching for miles, many of them hidden among the dense forest that still covered this part of the country. The lake was surrounded by trees – willows by the looks of them – which glowed a pale silver in the moonlight and rustled in the wind that animated their branches. Dan shivered and closed the window. When he finally fell asleep, his dreams were disturbing, alien.

A Tale of Two Sisters: First Night

The girl's beauty was spoken of even beyond the village boundaries. She could have had any of the local youths, but she chose the blacksmith's son. Her mother's bakery stood opposite the smithy, and she had frequently watched the young man helping his father shoe horses. While the blacksmith nailed on the iron shoes, his son tended the beasts, rubbing their tired legs and speaking to them gently. The couple fell in love, and their parents saw no reason to stand in the way of their happiness. Their wedding was not grand, but the whole village turned out, and the sun shone brightly for the bride and groom. But their joy was not to last long.

As was the custom, the lord of the manor had been invited to the wedding feast. As was his *custom, the lord had failed to turn up. Then, just as the sun was beginning to dip behind the trees, and the newlyweds were starting to wonder when they would be able to slip away from the festivities, the assembled villagers heard excited shouts and the sound of horses' hooves approaching rapidly.*

"Good evening!" It was the lord of the manor and a rowdy party of his companions. He jumped off his horse and his fellows followed suit. The villagers rose from the tables around which they were seated, bowing and curtsying to the newcomers. "We shan't be staying," informed the lord, "we've just come for the bride."

A stunned silence fell on the wedding party, broken only by the drunken guffaws of the lord's companions. The girl's already pale face turned as white as her bridal gown, and she looked to her husband for protection. The blacksmith's son stood rooted to the spot, and the lord addressed the girl.

"Don't look so frightened, my dear; I daresay we shan't do anything you haven't done before!"

"Please, my lord," a woman's voice rose from the crowd. "She's a good girl... A virgin." The lord was caught off guard for a moment, then spotted the girl's mother, and laughed.

"A virgin?"

118

"Yes, my lord." *The nobleman exchanged amused glances with his companions, then turned his attention back to the girl's mother.*

"All the better, woman. I'll teach her everything she needs to know to please her husband ... tomorrow night." The lord glanced at his cronies again, and they obliged with peels of raucous laughter.

"Please, my love," the girl took her husband's hand and whispered urgently to him as the young lord toyed with her mother. "Let's slip out the back. They're drunk. We'll take a horse and ride away. By tomorrow he'd have lost interest." Her husband looked at her sadly, but made no response. "Please, let's go. You are my only one. I'd rather die than lie with another."

"It is his right," the blacksmith's son finally replied. Those quietly spoken words shattered the girl's world. Tears welling up in her eyes, she pulled her hand from her husband's and fled from her wedding table. It took a moment for the lord to notice that his prize was gone.

"Well, what are you waiting for?" he shouted to his companions, angry and amused in equal measure. "Bring her back!"

The following morning, armed with a map and directions from the somewhat embarrassed receptionist, Henry and Dan set off in search of Henry's ancestral home. Henry seemed uncannily refreshed, considering how much vodka and how little sleep he'd had, and it was Dan who felt tired and uneasy. He still had vague memories of a bizarre dream he'd had – of the weeping willows that grew along the lake coming alive and forming a circle around him, trapping him and closing in on him. It was all he could do to keep up with his energetic friend.

The guesthouse that Henry had chosen – not that there was much choosing to do, it being the only one in the area – was not far from the manor house that had once belonged to Henry's ancestors. So the two young men set off on foot, following the road along the large lake. Dan avoided looking at the willows, gazing instead at the open fields on the opposite side of the road.

Eventually the lake curved away to the right. Henry and Dan kept to the road, and carried on straight ahead until they came across a large dilapidated stone gatepost to their left. A couple of metres away, obscured by brambles, stood a second gatepost.

"This is it," Henry grinned at Dan and turned off the road. As they passed between the two posts, they paused in wonder. Ahead of them stretched an avenue of ancient linden trees, seeming to go on forever. The friends exchanged awed glances, then headed up the avenue. Eventually they could make out a large grassy area with a circular grey stone structure in the distance, and beyond that the red bricks of a building. As Henry and Dan approached the end of the avenue, their excitement grew. Finally they were out of the shade of the trees and in the open: in what had once been a sizeable courtyard. Even now, overgrown with grass on which a cow was grazing, the courtyard was impressive. The stone structure in the centre of it was an old fountain – cracked and drained of water, the dry leaves inside it crackling in a breeze that stirred as the young men walked past. Something about the broken, empty structure unnerved Dan. Beyond the fountain and the courtyard stood the manor house. The render had long since fallen off, revealing the red brick that Henry and Dan had seen from the avenue. But the manor was still a thing of beauty. The main building was a vast rectangular block. On either side of it a curved colonnade led to a smaller, cube-like building. Together, the central block with its two wings formed a perfect horseshoe.

From what Henry had managed to find out while researching for their trip, the stately home was the work of an Italian architect – an unsung genius – who had been brought to Poland by a wealthy Polish count for the sole purpose of building him a palace fit for a king. The Italian had subsequently returned to Italy, where he was killed in a bar brawl in a village inn. The manor had since withstood attacks by Cossacks, Tartars and a variety of other hostile foreigners, before finally falling victim – in 1945 – to the Polish Communist Security Agency, whose

officers set fire to the main building on account of a unit of
anti-Communist Polish Home Army partisans hiding within its
walls. The partially burnt-out shell of the manor remained and, in
a humorously symbolic act of class-war – the intentionality of
which would never be known for sure – local representatives of
the Polish People's Workers' Party used it to house pigs. By the
1980s the porkers too were gone, and the manor remained in the
derelict state in which the two young Brits now found it. The
roof had caved in – in places, and here and there a shattered roof
tile lay upon the ground.

"So this belonged to your great grandfather?" asked Dan,
visibly impressed.

"And to his great grandfather before him," grinned Henry.
"You never know, with the Commies gone, maybe my dad can
claim it back or something!" Henry moved towards the main
entrance. "Come on!"

The front door was gone without a trace, and the two friends
entered slowly, careful not to fall down a hole – of which there
were many. There were piles of rubble lying around, the
obligatory quasi-Satanist graffiti on the walls, and two vast,
symmetrically positioned spiral staircases, but no banisters. After
an inspection of the ground floor rooms, which revealed the odd
partially standing chimney breast and more graffiti, the two
friends headed cautiously up the stairs. The first floor was
equally devastated, with bird droppings beneath the gaping holes
that had once been the windows. Dan was already slowly
mounting the stairs to the second floor, when Henry spotted a
doorway to a room that he hadn't noticed before.

"Go on up," he told Dan. "I'll be along in a minute. Just be
careful."

"Okay. You too."

The second floor laid bare the full extent of the damage to the
roof. It was dark here, despite the daylight outside, and, the
ceiling long being gone, shafts of light fell through the many
holes and cracks in the roof. Motes of dust danced and glistened
in the shafts, mesmerising Dan for a moment. Then, feeling
uneasy alone in the vast dark space, he moved cautiously to one

of the windows and peered out. He caught sight of movement and panicked on seeing figures in the park at the back of the building. He moved back a step – out of the light – but, on looking out again, realised that they were willow trees, hunched over like people. Unnerved, Dan called out to Henry, then went back down to the first floor to look for him.

"Henry?" No answer. Not finding him on the first floor, Dan carefully descended the less damaged spiral staircase. "Henry!" Dan figured that his friend must have gone back out – perhaps to explore the two wings of the palace – although Dan couldn't understand why he hadn't said anything.

But the buildings on either side of the main house were locked, and Henry was nowhere to be seen. There was only one place left to check, and that was the park behind the palace.

"Henry!" But there was no sign of Henry in the park either. As Dan turned back towards the manor, he thought he saw movement in one of the windows. "Oh, for God's sake... Henry!" Maybe his friend hadn't left the building after all, but then why hadn't he answered Dan's calls?

Dan walked quickly back to the house. There was no sign of anyone in the window now, but Dan was determined to go in for another look. As he reached the back of the house and started to head towards the colonnade, planning to cut through under its arches and go back into the house, he felt a sudden rush of air, then a sharp pain on the side of his head, and he was out cold.

Her heart was broken even before the dark waters closed over her head. She didn't struggle as her heavy garments took on water and pulled her down to the muddy bottom of the deep lake. She sank slowly – like a thousand broken-hearted maidens before her – and the willows wept beside her watery bed.

A brief moment of panic, as the girl's last breath escaped her; then a blissful stillness enveloped her, and a profound sense of serenity and peace.

Dan awoke to something wet and malodorous brushing against his face. The cow that had been grazing round the front of the manor house had wandered over and – whether for lack of salt in its diet or for some unfathomable bovine reason of its own – was now licking the prostrate young man. Dan jumped up and the startled cow beat a hasty retreat, mooing in alarm. Dan nearly blacked out again, and sat back down, breathing deeply. There was a dull throbbing pain in his temples and a much sharper pain at the side of his head when he touched it. He also had an impressive lump where the tile had struck. Unbeknown to Dan, his luck was in. Had the roof tile hit him full-on, rather than just skimming the side of his head, he would not be getting up again.

Dan shivered, and realised that the air had grown much colder – the sun was already going down. Alarmed at how much time must have passed, he called out to his friend. He suddenly felt afraid for Henry, but tried to console himself with the thought that Henry must have got carried away exploring somewhere in the house or vast grounds, and that he simply couldn't hear him calling. Dan got up – slowly this time – and made his way cautiously under the arches of the colonnade and back to the house, staying away from the eaves as much as he could.

Although the sun had not quite set, the shadows inside the manor were profound. Dan had planned to go all around the house again in search of his friend, but remembered the treacherous staircase and damaged floor, and thought better of it. Instead, he peered into the darkness from the threshold, and called Henry's name loudly. No response. Only the slight movement of shifting rubble somewhere in the depths of the building – too soft to be made by a man. Rats perhaps? Or just the house readjusting to the drop in temperature? But there was that feeling of dread in the pit of Dan's stomach again – fear of being left alone in this strange, abandoned place, but an even stronger fear for his friend.

"Henry!" Nothing. Dan touched his aching head gently, winced, then set off through the courtyard, hoping to do a large loop in front of the house before returning to the back and carrying out a thorough search of the gardens while there was still sufficient daylight. But as he walked past the fountain, something didn't seem right – something on the periphery of his vision. Dan stopped abruptly, and glanced to the right. That's when he saw the dark shape.

"Christ!" Dan's heart leapt in his chest, and for a moment he thought he might pass out again. He calmed himself as best he could, but the longer he stared at the thing in the fountain, the more details he noticed: the blue jeans, the navy sweatshirt, the dark blonde hair … yes, it was hair. There was no doubt now in Dan's mind. Lying in the cracked old fountain was a body, and the closer he got to it, the more certain he was that it was that of his friend.

A rough, scratching sensation roused the girl from her murky grave. She felt a sharp tug, then another and another. Then coarse limbs were holding her, and gnarled digits curled around her body. She was being lifted, pulled and dragged – upwards and out and away from the death-bringing, peace-bringing water.

As she felt solid ground beneath her feet once more, the girl's feet began to crack. On all sides the willow trees that cradled her started to grow over and into and through her body. Roots moved through her legs and feet, shackling her to the earth. Her fingers grew long and brittle; her skin hardened, thickened and erupted in shoots and stems, which shivered in the evening air. The girl tried to move, but her legs were rooted to the spot and her torso trapped in a wooden corset that held her fast. Her eyes became hollow, her throat twisted and dry. She screamed, and her cry froze forever onto the rugged bark of her lips.

All memories fled the girl, bar those of sadness and longing, betrayal and anger, and a need for revenge stronger than hunger or thirst – stronger than the centuries that would come and go.

The minutes and days that followed could only be described as a never-ending nightmare… Touching his friend's ice-cold neck to check for a pulse; the glazed, milky eye that stared up at him from under Henry's matted hair; stumbling back to the guesthouse through the dark. Then the uncomprehending, shocked face of the receptionist; the police; the ambulance; the battery of questions and suspicious looks. But the worst thing was seeing Henry's parents: his mother trembling like a leaf in a gale, his father ashen-faced and trying to be strong for his wife.

"What happened, Dan?"

"I don't know. I ... don't ... know."

Dan went over the events of that day a hundred times – with Henry's parents, with the police, when he lay awake at night. But nobody would ever know why it was that Henry's lungs were filled with water or how it was that a young man could drown in the long-empty shell of a cracked old fountain.

By the time the men reached the lake, there was no sign of the girl, just the tattered remains of a white dress hanging from a willow tree on the bank. The girl's corpse was never found, which came as no surprise – the lake was deep; its murky depths hid many a broken body and shattered dream. But four weeks later the lord of the manor was discovered – face down in his own fountain. And by the time the first snow covered the ground like wedding lace, the hapless blacksmith's son was dead too. The doctor who examined his body refused to comment, but the villagers whispered that the young man's face was twisted with terror and that clenched tightly in his fist was a single green-leafed sprig of willow. But surely these were just rumours – after all, willows shed their leaves long before winter falls...

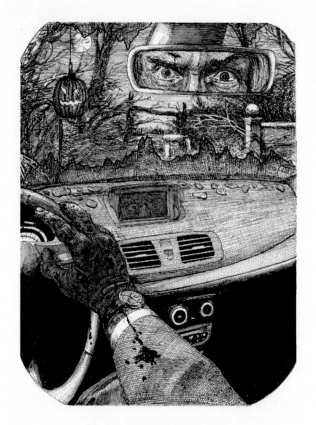

HALLOWEEN LIGHTS

Where am I? The dark road, the bushes and trees on either side, shrouded in mist, all look the same. I strain my eyes, searching the night for something familiar – something I can grasp. Then the road bends slightly, dips a little, and that's when I see the light. It has a warm, orange glow and I know that I must reach it. If I reach the light, everything will be okay.

I stagger through the mist, trying to remember what happened. A cold wind tugs at the branches of the trees and scatters the autumn leaves. I sense movement behind me and spin round, but see nothing. I hurry towards the light, confused as it fragments into a thousand glimmering specks, dancing on the horizon.

How long have I been walking? The leaves crunch beneath my feet as I hasten along the side of the road. Then a twig snaps behind me. I stop abruptly and hear a leaf rustle before silence falls. I look round. Is that a shadow, a darker shade of black against the night? I step up my pace, desperate now to reach the light.

Walking, I hear sounds behind me. When I stop, they stop. When I move forward, they start up again. I hurry on, sure I feel eyes burning into my back.

I break into a run, not slowing until I reach the edge of town. As I head towards the houses, I see the source of the points of light. Not what I expected. They shimmer in a hundred carved pumpkins, orange teeth casting strange dark shapes on the wood of porches and the grey wetness of paving-stone.

The shadow behind me forgotten, I wonder at the intricate forms of dark and light dancing before my eyes. Not sure now which way to go – like a moth that believes itself soaring towards the moon, only to find itself trapped in a house full of dusty light bulbs. I pause awhile, unsure what to do next.

I cringe as a shriek pierces the night, and footsteps grow and echo in my ears. Excited voices are coming closer. I cower behind a tree, uncertain. The trick-or-treaters pass and I breathe easy.

I move on and hear that crunch of trampled leaves behind me. The shadow – how could I have forgotten the shadow? I scour the street and think I see movement in the bushes to the right. I move off fast.

More youths approach. I look for somewhere to hide, but it's too late. They're upon me, laughing and shouting. "Nice costume!" I lower my eyes and keep moving. They pass by, staring.

From all around, the twinkling lights distract me once more and my mind wanders. I can't remember how I got here. I recall walking along the side of the road, with trees and bushes on either side. I close my eyes for a moment and try to see with my mind's eye. Glimpses of road, of trees and bushes, but they rush by so quickly – I'm not walking, I'm driving. Of course – my car. The '69 Chevy convertible that I lovingly restored with my own hands, smoothing every screw, every piece of metal into its rightful place. It took me five years of weekends to turn the rusted hulk into a thing of beauty – its cerulean blue and white more worthy of an angel than of an ungainly, un-special man like me.

Where is my car? Now I remember: I had to leave my car behind. So that's what I'm doing – I'm looking for a phone to get some help out to my car. My cell phone is gone; I must have lost it getting out of the Chevy. I can't remember. I must focus. I can't be standing here in the middle of the road.

A scream brings me out of my reverie and I look down at a whimpering child dressed as a ghost, its face as pale as the sheet that's draped over its body. It drops the plastic jack-o'-lantern it is carrying and wails at me, its body trembling. I reach down to comfort it, but the child's mother pulls it away, cursing me loudly.

Two teenage boys and a girl run past. The girl is wearing small, red devil's horns. She reminds me of someone – someone I loved or love still, someone I should remember. Broken images of a woman's smile form in my mind; of bright green eyes and a wisp of dark blonde hair blowing in the wind as fields and trees stream by behind her. I struggle to put the shattered pieces together, but the boys' shouting dispels the fledgling vision and plastic severed limbs are waved in front of my face before the teens disappear down a side street.

What am I doing? A cat hisses at me from across the street and I move on. Where am I going? Ah yes, I'm going to find a house – so many to choose from – and ring a doorbell. And then what? I'm ringing a doorbell, but the sound of movement inside makes me panic. I can't remember what it was that I wanted.

I run behind the house and listen as the homeowner looks up and down the street and says "Hello? ... Anybody there?" before going back in and locking the door. I grasp desperately at bits of thoughts; I search my mind for what I'm meant to be doing, for where I'm meant to be, but all around me the lights flicker and purr, and pumpkin eyes are mesmerising, disorientating. Where am I?

I remember – my car. I need to call a garage to get my Chevy off the side of the road and get it fixed so that I can drive to the girl with the dark blonde hair and green eyes... Alice. Alice is waiting for me at her parents' house. We are supposed to see a double bill at the local cinema: *Halloween* and *Friday the Thirteenth*. Or is it *The Evil Dead* and *The Fog*?

I struggle with the mist that's rising before me, getting into my eyes and obscuring the lights. What am I doing? Focus ... oh yes. I need to find a house and ring a doorbell. I need to phone a garage and get the Chevy fixed so I can take Alice to see *The Texas Chainsaw Massacre*. Or is it *The Exorcist*?

I concentrate hard and push the mist away. I walk to the house with the largest number of pumpkins lining the steps. Here the mist is weakest – the lights are fighting it, keeping it at bay. I ring the doorbell.

The woman's smile fades; she looks startled. But then she smiles again. "Your costume," she tells me, "it's very ... gruesome... And aren't you a little old to be trick-or-treating?"

I open my mouth to speak, but I forget what it is that I want to say. I rack my brain... Alice... Alice ... the woman turns away. A tear runs down my cheek.

The woman returns, holding a box of chocolates. I can't recall. I raise my hand, pleading for patience, pleading for her to wait while I remember, pleading for help.

The woman's face changes. "What's that smell?" A distressed grimace distorts her mouth. The box slips from her hand and chocolates fall in all directions. She is staring at my extended hand. And then she starts to scream.

I follow the woman's gaze. My hand has burst into flames – orange and yellow – licking up my arm. I look down at my body. I am a mass of open wounds and charred flesh. Still I burn.

The mist thickens before my eyes until I no longer see the screaming woman. A wind starts to blow, whipping the mist into a spinning, howling vortex. Cold arms envelop me, holding me steady, strangely soothing against my burning skin. The shadow is whispering in my ear, telling me not to scream, telling me that nerve endings have burnt away and it doesn't really hurt. "Hush now. It won't be much longer."

I hurtle through the mist. The wind howls a crescendo and stops suddenly. There is a jolt. My muscles spasm – like that second between sleeping and waking, when you think you've been falling, but when you finally crash it's into your own soft, familiar bed, and you never really fell at all. The mist clears. For the briefest moment all is still, and then the burning begins again.

I'm in my Chevy, speared to my seat by blackened metal. My hand burns on the steering-wheel, my body burns in my seat. My world is flame. I open my mouth to scream, but the shadow's words resound in my ears. I look up and see it watching me through the windscreen. Behind it there is light. Not the distracting orange glow that led me astray, but brilliant white light. Light that I long for more than anything in the world ... anything except perhaps ... Alice...

THE COFFIN

Jack lived a stone's throw from the rear gate of the cemetery, so it made perfect sense for him to cut through the vast necropolis to get to the tube. Jack wasn't particularly fond of cemeteries – not like those people who took photos of derelict graveyards or paid good money to visit burial grounds with famous residents. He'd certainly never planned to live near one, but when his childless aunt died and left him her house, he wasn't going to look the proverbial gift horse in the mouth. And the walk through the cemetery wasn't altogether unpleasant. So the fifteen minutes cut from Jack's commute to work – and another fifteen minutes from his trek back again – made it worth having to walk

131

past all those dead people, and occasional living ones too. The worst was when there was a funeral on. Jack hated that. It made him feel like an interloper – intruding on people's private grief. So whenever he saw a priest and a group of mourners at a freshly dug grave, he would slope past and out of the cemetery even quicker than usual.

Today was no exception. As Jack hurried along the central avenue to the main gate at the far end, he saw a coffin some way away from the path he was traversing. A furtive glance told him that, although the coffin was positioned next to a freshly dug grave, there were no mourners or gravediggers nearby. Strange for a coffin to be left unattended like that. Perhaps the mourners had already left and the gravediggers hadn't arrived yet. Jack hastened through the cemetery, out the main gate and across the road to the underground station. From there the tube ferried him – with two changes along the way – to the offices of Lidell and Lidell, where he worked as an administrator.

Jack forgot all about the coffin – until, that is, he was on his way home and striding through the cemetery once more. This time he could afford a more leisurely pace. The sun was beginning to set, but the cemetery wouldn't close for at least another hour. Jack relished the last of the day's sunshine; the air had a pleasant temperature despite the days already getting shorter. Then something caught his eye: something glinting in the setting sun. It stood on the edge of the grass verge, almost spilling out onto the central avenue. Whatever it was, it stood between Jack and the rear gate, and, unless he took a detour, which would involve weaving in and out of the tombstones and crosses, he would have to walk right past it. Jack slowed down and squinted myopically in the direction of the large, pallid object. As he got closer, he wondered why it had taken him so long to recognise the elongated hexagonal form. It was a coffin, carved in a pale wood, which just now glowed as it caught the sun's last rays. Then it was plunged into a dim half-light, as dusk fell quickly.

A coffin in a cemetery – not really a combination to be wondered at, and yet something about the casket made Jack nervous. Not only was it placed far too close to the path – almost pushing out onto it – but, Jack finally realised, it was the same coffin he'd seen earlier in the day. Still unattended, but in a different position than when he'd been rushing to work. Weird. But not weird enough to make him turn back and take the long way home. Jack decided not to take a detour along a different path through the cemetery either, but scurried on, as far from the casket as the wide central avenue would allow, eyes fixed firmly on the path ahead.

As he scuttled past the coffin and on towards the exit gate, Jack became aware of his own heartbeat. Once he estimated that he was past the offending container, he released the breath he hadn't realised he'd been holding. After twenty more metres or so, Jack slowed down. He planned to reach the exit gate without looking back, but then decided that he was being stupid. Aiming to put his mind at ease, he paused and turned around, nearly jumping out of his skin at what he saw. The coffin was no longer at the edge of the central avenue: it was right in the middle of it, and only ten metres or so from where Jack was standing. It was a trick of the light – he thought; a case of false perspective. There was no one around to move the coffin and therefore the coffin could not have moved.

But as Jack set off rapidly for the exit once more, he cast another glance behind him. And this time there was no mistaking it: the distance between him and the pale-coloured casket had shrunk by at least a couple of metres.

Jack ran for the gate, his heart pounding fiercely in his chest. He never saw the coffin move, but each time he glanced over his shoulder, the horrid object had gained a little more ground. Finally Jack was nearing the exit gate, but as it came into full view his prayers that the caretaker hadn't locked it early dwindled to a hoarse whimper: the gate was shut.

"Oh God!" Jack threw himself at the gate and rattled it vigorously. It swung open. "Thank you!" Not locked; just closed – probably by some overzealous visitor on his or her way out. Without looking back, Jack slammed the gate shut behind him and darted for the safety of his front door, all the while telling himself that he hadn't just heard the scrape of wood on paving stone.

A couple of large vodkas and several cautious glances out of the window later, Jack managed to convince himself that he'd imagined the entire coffin episode. After all, with the audit and everything else that was going on at work, he hadn't been sleeping at all well lately. And everyone knows that the mind plays tricks – especially on the sleep-deprived and in that strange half-light between day and dusk. Perhaps the shortcut through the graveyard was not such a good idea after all. Maybe he should bite the bullet and start going the long way around. Particularly now that darkness was falling earlier. Besides, the extra walk would do him good. The paunch he was starting to grow didn't hang well on his otherwise skinny frame.

After a microwave dinner and a couple of hours' television, Jack drank a final shot of vodka and called it a day. The alcohol knocked him out for an hour or two, but then he woke with a start. Afraid for no apparent reason, he reached for the bedside light, but a sudden noise at the far side of his room startled him and he jerked his arm in alarm, knocking the flimsy lamp off the small cabinet.

"Shit!" The crash as the lamp hit the floor told Jack that the bulb had probably smashed, but in any case, he had no time to find out, as the shuffling, scraping sound came again, this time closer than before. "Oh God!" Jack froze, and just then the waxing moon emerged from behind a cloud, casting enough light into the bedroom to propel Jack's fear to a new level.

Incomprehension and terror fought for control of Jack's mind as he tried to make sense of what he was seeing. It was standing at the foot of his bed, glimmering a pale silvery blue in the moonlight. The bedroom door and window were closed. In any case, the damned thing would not have fit through the window, and there was no sign of broken glass.

Jack had to get out of the bedroom. Out of the house. Without taking his eyes off the casket, he tried to pull off his duvet and swing his legs out of bed, but found himself no longer master of his own body. As he finally succeeded merely in clenching his fists into tight, painful balls, the coffin at the foot of his bed started to groan and creak in a most alarming way. The pallid wood splintered and, as Jack watched, speechless, a clawed hand thrust its way heavenward from the hideous box, followed by another, and then the planks of the coffin were being pushed apart with inhuman strength, splinters raining down and nails popping out like champagne corks on New Year's Eve.

Jack couldn't move and he couldn't look away from the abomination that pulled itself nimbly out of the shattered wood and hissed at him through large yellow teeth that tapered to razor-sharp points. Its bloodshot eyes bored into Jack's, rooting him to the spot like an animal caught in the headlights of an approaching juggernaut. The cold metal slats of the headboard pressed into Jack's back as he pushed himself as far away as he could from the fetid, hairless monstrosity that now lurched towards him.

And as the fiend's foul stench enveloped him, Jack finally managed to close his eyes, the scream cut short in his throat as the creature's fangs sank in.

Jack hadn't missed a day's work in nine years, so when he didn't show up at the office for three days or answer any phone calls, his concerned boss contacted the police.

The officers had never seen such a hideous expression of terror on anyone's face. There was an infected wound on the victim's neck, and the body had been drained of blood. Even before the police pathologist was called in, Inspector Dougall knew that the case would never be solved. There were no signs of forced entry, and nothing appeared to be out of place. Only a large pile of pale, splintered, rotting wood at the foot of the hapless man's bed.

THE CREAKING

Alice hurried through the forest, her basket filled with fresh herbs, and small pots of strengthening tonics and soothing balms. She had worked all night, crushing healing leaves and seeds, grinding nourishing roots and dried fungi; mixing her concoctions so that she could bring relief to the sick and ailing as soon as the sun was up.

Partially hidden by trees and thicket, her little house was a good half-hour walk from the village. It would have been easier if people came to her rather than her having to go to them, but some of those she helped were old and frail, others were very sick or busy looking after small children. Besides, the villagers didn't seem keen on walking through the forest, even during the day. This was something Alice couldn't understand. For her, the forest meant sanctuary and nurture: it hid her from the madding crowd, and provided her with food and all the plants she needed to mix her medicines and make a meagre living. And what didn't grow in the forest grew in the marshes and fields nearby.

Alice hadn't been blessed with attractive features or an easy life. Her father had died when she was a little girl, and her mother had raised her alone. From an early age, she had learnt how to heal, and how to survive by working hard and keeping herself to herself. Alice's mother had traded remedies for eggs, milk, flour and the occasional piece of cloth to patch up clothes, and now Alice did the same.

Going to the village had been a frightening experience even when her mother was alive, but in the five years since her mother's death it just seemed to get harder. The villagers stared at her: adults whispered behind her back and children called her names. Even the people whom she helped were uneasy around her. They were grateful enough for the relief her remedies brought, but Alice could sense that as soon as she'd applied the ointment they needed or handed over their medicine, they didn't like her hanging around.

The only bearable part of going to the village was the walk through the forest. Of course, Alice was in the forest practically every day collecting berries, fungi, herbs or kindling for the fire, but she loved spending time in the woods without having to 'work'. When she was strolling among the ancient trees, listening to the birds and the soft, startled noises of small creatures scurrying away in the undergrowth, she felt something akin to contentment.

Today was no different, except for the fact that Alice couldn't take her time; she needed to get to the village as soon as possible – Maggie Gray was counting on her to help her ailing daughter. The toddler had been coughing for several days now, and none of the usual mixtures of honey and herbs had worked. Alice had had to resort to mixing a blend based heavily on coltsfoot, and that had to be prepared in just the right way or it could poison the little girl rather than heal her. The sooner she could administer the medicine, the greater the chance that the child would recover. So Alice hurried along the path that wound its way to the village.

It was early morning and the sunlight was just beginning to filter down through the trees, but even at high noon the forest floor would be dark – the tall and leafy trees casting a permanent shadow. At her brisk pace Alice couldn't hear the birdsong that she usually enjoyed. Today her footsteps accompanied her, and the occasional flurry of wings as a bird fled its nest in alarm.

As Alice burst out into the clearing not far from her home, she came face to face with a young deer. Alice froze, her face breaking into a smile, and gazed at the creature in wonder. No matter how many times she came across deer in the forest, their regal grace never failed to bring her joy.

The animal held Alice's gaze, its mouth moving impassively as it chewed its morning meal. Then a loud creaking sound rang out behind Alice. The deer bolted in fright, disappearing into the undergrowth, and Alice spun round, but saw nothing. She stood very still, her heartbeat hard and fast. The sound came again: the wrenching, squealing, rasping sound of wood being stretched and distorted. Again and again the creaking resounded, as if a tree were being pummelled and bent by a strong wind, yet not the slightest hint of a breeze stirred in the forest. Alice wanted to run, but her legs refused to oblige. Instead, she peered into the trees, trying to see what was causing the heavy, rhythmic creak. It sounded like something was exerting a considerable amount of pressure on a large branch, but Alice saw nothing. Struggling to conquer her fear, she placed her basket on the ground and took a step towards the sound. As she did so, the sound stopped. Alice moved forward a few paces, and the sound came again – this time right above her head. Alice screamed. She grabbed her basket and ran.

Alice kept running until her strength ran out, then stopped and looked fearfully behind her. Of course there was nothing there; what could there possibly be? As her breath slowed and her heart stilled enough for her to hear the forest around her, Alice strained her ears for the horrible sound. She heard only the wind in the trees and bushes, and the stirring of the wildlife around her, and yet the grating, jarring creaking reverberated in her head. She knew instinctively that nothing would be capable of wiping that sound from her mind. The trees and bushes around her appeared darker; the soft, familiar sounds of creatures moving through the undergrowth seemed sinister, unnerving. For the first time in her life, the forest was no longer a haven, no longer a friend; it was something to be feared. Alice realised that her fear was out of all proportion to what had happened, and yet it persisted.

That day, Alice spent as little time in the village as she could, explaining to people how to use the tinctures, balsams and poultices she had prepared for them, rather than staying to administer them. She even turned down Maggie Gray's offer of a meal, although she did stay long enough to show the mother how to dose the cough mixture for her little girl. Instead, Alice packed away the food and other items that the villagers gave her in return for her services, and hurried home, going out of her way to avoid the clearing with the large creaking tree at its edge. She made sure that she gathered everything she needed for the next day long before darkness fell, then locked herself away in her house. But try as she might, she couldn't get the creaking out of her head.

That night Alice dreamt that she was running through the forest. It was dark, and something blacker than the night was chasing her. As she ran, nettles stung her, thorns scratched her, and roots tried to trip her up and send her sprawling. Alice ran blindly on and unexpectedly found herself bursting out into the clearing. She came to an abrupt halt, shocked at finding herself exposed and vulnerable to the dark malignant presence that pursued her. She moved swiftly, but silently back into the trees and listened for any sound of her pursuer. And that's when it came: the bloodcurdling screech of bending wood – the creaking that turned the sweat on Alice's back to ice. She spun round, looking up into the large tree above her. Was that a black shape –

a shadow crouching in the branches? Alice screamed and woke up.

For the next few days Alice continued to avoid the clearing and the tree, but her unease didn't lessen. If anything, it grew. She gathered what plants she needed for her medicines without straying any further from her house than she had to, she did her rounds in the village and hurried back home. At night she dreamt about the darkness that pursued her through the forest, and the creaking. Then one day when she got to the village, she found the villagers in a tense and morose mood. The Tyrell boy had gone missing. His abusive and permanently angry father had last seen him the night before. Old man Tyrell had been drinking in the kitchen with his friends when the boy came in to say goodnight.

"Fuck off to bed, you little shit!" Tyrell's response elicited peals of laughter from his drunken cronies.

The boy had scuttled off to bed, and that was the last anyone had seen of him. Old man Tyrell had woken up at lunchtime and gone round the house, looking for someone to vent his hangover on. He couldn't find his twelve-year-old son, so he clouted his wife, and demanded to be fed. Mrs Tyrell had gone out into the yard to call Tommy in for lunch, assuming that he'd got up early, made his own breakfast and gone to play with friends. But her son was nowhere to be seen.

"I can't find Tommy," she told her husband as she fearfully set his plate of food down in front of him.

"I'll kill the little shit when he gets back," he had replied.

Tyrell spent the afternoon drinking, only pausing between drinks to repeat his threat, but by the time it got dark and his wife had unsuccessfully scoured the village for the boy, his protestations had decreased somewhat in their vehemence, if not frequency. A brief torch-lit search of the village and its immediate surroundings was organised, but Tommy wasn't found.

The villagers quickly did what villagers often do in times of perceived threat: they became suspicious and mistrustful of outsiders. It was into this atmosphere that Alice arrived the next morning. She checked in on the little Gray girl and gave Maggie a fresh pot of medicine for her. The toddler's cough had lessened.

"She's getting better," Alice smiled shyly at Maggie Gray.

"Yes." Maggie pulled her daughter towards herself, away from Alice, then got a hold of herself and added without much enthusiasm, "Thank you, Alice." There was an uncomfortable silence.

"I'll be going then," offered Alice, adding nervously, "Mrs Pratt is waiting for her bunion ointment." Maggie got up silently and fetched a dozen eggs from the back of the house.

Mrs Pratt was in a talkative mood. Alice was hardly through the door, when the old woman told her how Tommy had disappeared the day before and how a search of the village had turned up no sign of him.

"Poor Betty Tyrell is hysterical," Mrs Pratt said with barely concealed delight, "and even old man Tyrell has been out looking for the boy."

"That's terrible," responded Alice. "I hope they find him.

Tommy had risen early the day before, grabbed a slice of bread and a piece of cheese, and crept out of the house without waking his parents. He'd decided on the previous night that he would visit his cousin in the neighbouring village. There was no point asking his parents, as his mother would defer to his father, and his father would hit him with the buckle of his belt. If he slipped out early, he could get back by teatime. His father would be too hung-over in the morning and too drunk in the afternoon to notice that he was gone, and he would be home for supper.

The boy set out across the cornfields just as dawn broke, and was at his cousin's in time for breakfast. Charlie was thrilled to see him, and his aunt and uncle made a fuss of him.

"Your parents do know you're here?" questioned his aunt.

Tommy nodded, "Uh-huh."

"And they let you come all the way here on your own?"

"Uh-huh." Tommy smiled at his uncle and aunt. He was jealous of Charlie. Charlie's dad never hit him or shouted at his mother. Charlie's mum was pretty and always smiling; not like Tommy's mother, who had frown lines and puffy tear-stained eyes, and was always sad.

Charlie's father helped the boys to make fishing rods, whilst his mother made them a hamper with bread, cheese, ham and milk, and then the two cousins set out for the river. The day was warm and sultry; the boys fished and chatted, ate and eventually dozed off in a haystack, waking up when the sun started going down and a chill crept into the air. By the time they got back to Charlie's house, there was less than an hour of daylight left. As Tommy had a two-hour walk to get home, his uncle and aunt offered to let him stay the night, provided his parents wouldn't be worried. Tommy told them that his parents had said he could stay over if it got late and could come home on Sunday. He would get a hiding one way or another, so he figured he might as well delay the inevitable.

When Tommy got home, his mother ran to him and hugged him, tears of relief staining her face. "Where have you been?"

Tommy's father was sitting at the kitchen table, surrounded by his drinking cronies, who were helping him drown his sorrows and work out where to look for his boy. Before Tommy had time to answer his mother, his father got up from the table and lumbered towards him.

"I'm gonna kill you, you little shit!" Tommy didn't know whether to stay or run. He'd rarely seen his father quite so angry. "Where the devil have you been, you little shit?" Tommy cowered back as his father approached, pulling off his belt and brandishing the buckle end at his son. "Go on, tell me! Where have you been, you little shit?" The belt whistled through the air and hit the boy on the side, knocking him off his feet. His mother screamed and ran to defend her son, but Tyrell pushed her out of the way and went to take another swing at the boy. There must have been a particularly homicidal look on old man Tyrell's face, as his companions stopped laughing, and one of them decided to intervene. Jim pulled himself up drunkenly from the kitchen table, and staggered up between Tyrell and his son.

"Witch took you, did she, boy? Witch took you ... to make a potion out of your blood?"

Old man Tyrell paused, belt in hand, confused by the question.

"Witch took you and locked you up, but you got away?" prompted Jim.

"I'll kill you, you little shit!" Tyrell had regained his momentum and was about to pelt the boy again, when Tommy piped up from the floor, "Yes, sir."

"Huh?" grunted Tyrell.

"Witch took me and locked me up, but I got away."

"Who locked you up?" fumed Tyrell. "Are you lying to me, boy?"

"No, sir."

"If you're lying to me, I'll kill you!"

"Witch took me and ... was gonna ... make me into a potion ... but I got away."

"Nobody hurts my boy!" Tyrell turned to face his friends. "You hear me? Nobody hurts *my* boy!"

"We hear you, Robert." Jim raised his hand in a placating gesture, but there was no placating old man Tyrell.

"I'll kill her! I'll kill the witch!" Tyrell glared at his companions. "Are you going to sit there or are you going to help me?"

As old man Tyrell was the parish constable, they decided to help.

"Who's he talking about?" Nathaniel Jackson whispered as the drunken party spilled out of the house after Tyrell.

"Alice Goodman, I guess," mused George Hogge. "Ain't no one else around here makes potions."

"Hang on, Robert!" Jim tried to undo what he'd done, but it was too late. He was pushed aside, and by the time old man Tyrell had finished rousing the villagers, his party was over a dozen strong. They set off to put an end to the witch who'd been killing children, draining their blood and grinding up their bones to make her unholy potions. Old Joe had been living in the village for a long time, and knew exactly how to get to the witch's house.

Alice had just cleaned up after supper, and was getting ready to mix her medicines for the following day, when she heard the voices. At first she thought she must be mistaken, but the shouting grew louder, angrier. And now she could see the flickering orange light of torches dancing amongst the trees. They were getting closer, and Alice knew she should run, but it was too late, they were already here. A baying mob shrieking and snarling like beasts.

"Alice Goodman, come out! Come out now or we're coming in!"

Alice stood rooted to the spot with fear. Then the door flew open and Robert Tyrell burst in, accompanied by his own personal lynch mob. Alice wanted to scream, but no sound came from her throat.

"Gotcha, you fucking witch!" growled Tyrell.

"You won't be killing no more children!" someone shouted from the back of the crowd. Alice couldn't speak, but she shook her head and held up her hands in a vain attempt to ward off the fury that was being hurled at her. Then Tyrell had her by the hair, and she was twisting in pain, being forced out into the night, fists punching her and nails scratching her, as she was half-dragged, half-carried out of her house and through the forest.

A punch to Alice's right eye screwed it tight shut as the tissue swelled up around it. Her left eye filled with her own blood from a gash on her forehead. She couldn't see, and in her fear and pain she couldn't sense that the trees around her had thinned and the undergrowth had given way to grass.

"This'll do!" someone shouted. Alice recognised the voice of John Briggs. Only last week she'd cured the fungal infection on his feet with her garlic and chamomile ointment. He said he'd never forget what she'd done for him. The villagers stopped, and Alice tried to cry out to Briggs, but still no sound came from her cracked, bleeding lips. Alice threw herself forward in an attempt to break free. A violent tug to her hair ripped much of it out and brought on a fresh wave of pain.

"Stay still, witch!" It was Tyrell's voice. "Hold her, will you!"

"Give it here!" shouted Briggs.

Rough hands held her even tighter, crushing her arms. Then Alice felt something being pulled down over her head. She realised what was about to happen moments before she felt the rope sting and tighten around her neck. Then she was being hoisted off her feet, the burning pain in her neck unbearable and the breath choked out of her slowly, prolonging her agony.

The last thing Alice heard was the horrific, jarring creaking as the branch bent under her weight and the darkness took her.

DIRTY DYBBUK

*630,720,000 seconds without sex. And each of those seconds like
a lifetime. For time has no meaning in the abyss. Hundreds of
years can go by in a moment or a second can drag out for a
thousand years. And that's a long time to go without sex. A very
long time.*

'Boys don't make passes at girls who wear glasses.' The less
than friendly expression had stuck in Mitzi's mind since primary
school so that, when her likewise short-sighted friends moved on
to contact lenses, Mitzi wore her thick-framed spectacles with

146

added determination. For Mitzi had no intention of having passes made at her by boys. Absolutely no way.

Mitzi was almost twenty-one now and studying English at Oxford University. Sadly there were no women's colleges left; the last one – St. Hilda's – had opted to admit men in 2006 – a financial necessity rather than a matter of equality and fraternity. So Mitzi frequented New College – one of the oldest colleges in the university – where she was a dedicated member of the Jewish Society and the Women's Group. At the end of every term, Mitzi would return home to Golders Green – the leafy and pleasant part of London in which she'd lived all her life.

It wasn't that Mitzi disliked boys or that she was a lesbian – God forbid. Not at all. But Mitzi came from a good family – a respectable, middle class family – and when the time was right for her to marry, her parents would ask a *shadkhan* to pick out a suitable young man for her.

The abyss was long and deep. Inside it were chained the angels that had rebelled against the Lord. Some of them had taken human women as their brides and fathered giants that ransacked the earth. The lust and suffering of the trapped angels drew her to the abyss, but the flames that raged there barred all entry. She floated through the forbidden places, but always made her way back to the human realm. How she envied the women their flesh, with the infinite capacity for pleasure that it brought. How it angered her seeing prudish schoolgirls and pious old maids who kept their legs together and shunned the touch of men. They didn't deserve the soft skin and the heaven between their thighs that had been so brutally snatched from her. Some spark of consciousness within the hungry tormented spirit that was once human drove her relentlessly to her earthly roots. The ties that bind drew her inexorably back to those whose flesh was of her own. And after twenty years of torment that only a disembodied nymphomaniac could understand, she finally found the home that she'd been longing for.

Mitzi had been feeling light-headed the night before and had gone to bed early. She awoke suddenly at dawn as a jolt of energy shot through her body. Startled and confused, she sat up and looked around the room. Then she remembered: it was her birthday! She was going shopping with her best friend, and later her parents were taking her out to dinner at *Six 13* – her very favourite restaurant. But something was not quite right. She was feeling tense in an odd, albeit rather pleasant sort of way, and her thoughts turned inexplicably to the blonde blue-eyed *goy* from her staircase in New College. Mark – that was his name. Mitzi tried to push the image of the young man's muscular form from her mind and fought hard against the strange sensations that were taking over her body. But she was battling a will stronger than her own, and soon she closed her eyes and sank back onto her pillow, her hand straying downwards beneath the sheets.

The girl had put up an impressive struggle, but she was young and ripe, and in the end susceptible. The joy of having such a lovely firm body to exploit was indescribable. She was almost able to forget that this fine youthful frame wasn't her own. And there were so many men out there, and so much pleasure to be had.

'Rise and shine with Night Light glow in the dark condoms'. For Hannah Goldblatt the shopping trip had become a surrealist nightmare. She had gladly agreed to accompany Mitzi – her closest friend since primary school – to check out a few shops on the Finchley Road. The idea was to help Mitzi choose some clothes for her summer term at Oxford, and break up the hard work of shopping with a bite to eat at *Daniel's Bagel Bakery*. But no – at the last minute Mitzi had insisted that they go to Camden Market, catching Hannah off guard, and using the fact that it was her birthday to bully her friend into going along with her heinous plan. And not only were they now far from home, surrounded by Goths, drug dealers and overexcited tourists, but they were standing in front of the *Sex Emporium*, an unhealthy glint in Mitzi's eye.

"Let's go," pleaded Hannah. The unfamiliar area made her nervous and more than a little frightened, and she was convinced that everyone who walked past was staring at the two unhip Jewish girls in front of the adult store.

"You go if you want," Mitzi told Hannah, "I'm going in." And she did. Hannah looked around fearfully, spotted three youths in black leather jackets across the road, and hurried in after her friend.

An hour later, a traumatised Hannah emerged from the sex shop with a dazed expression, carrying the bags that Mitzi was too overloaded to manage on her own: bags of kinky nurse and nun outfits, edible undies, a *Rampant Rabbit* and curry-flavoured condoms.

"I'm thirsty." Mitzi smiled warmly at her pale and silent friend. "Let's go to the pub."

"You can't go out dressed like that!" Mitzi had come downstairs in her new tight black miniskirt, high-heeled shoes and clinging low-cut red top, and was now facing down her shocked parents in a scene reminiscent of an old Western.

"It's *my* birthday," she stated firmly. A compromise was finally reached in the form of a cardigan that covered the top half of Mitzi's assets, and the family party left for dinner, but the atmosphere during the meal remained tense.

Over the next few weeks, the relationship between Mitzi and her once doting parents continued to deteriorate, as the young woman took to staying out late and coming home stinking of alcohol, with her lipstick smudged and bits of grass stuck to the back of her jacket. The last straw came in the form of a Thursday evening phone call from the next-door neighbour. Mitzi's mother answered the phone.

"Vera," Mrs Rosenberg said coldly. "I don't know quite how to say this, but I'm afraid you have to do something about your daughter."

"What do you mean?"

"Simcha is only sixteen."

"What are you saying?"

"I'm saying that Mitzi's been flashing over the garden fence."
"Flashing?"
"Her ... boobies."

Mitzi had been feeling restless all morning. There'd been no post, so no postman to flirt with, and no prospect of any male company all day. It was very warm for late April, and Mitzi sat in the garden, trying to read a college textbook. Then she heard voices – young male voices – and remembered the kid next door. Without even realising that she'd stood up, Mitzi found herself peering over the garden fence. She had the distinct feeling that something bad was going to happen, and she tried to turn around and go back to her deckchair, but it was too late.

"Hi, Simcha," she heard herself say.

"Hi, Mitzi." Simcha smiled and walked over to the fence.

"Who's your friend?" She grinned past Simcha at the freckly teenager seated at the outdoor table, sipping a fizzy drink.

"Oh, that's Aaron."

"Hi Aaron," said Mitzi, feeling increasingly nervous and trying hard to find a way to end the conversation.

"Hi," the boy waved.

"Would you boys like to see something?" Mitzi asked.

"Sure," Aaron got up and joined Simcha at the fence. And that's when it happened: before she knew it, Mitzi had her top hoisted all the way up over her naked breasts, the fear and excitement overwhelming as the boys stared, then giggled, then turned and fled as Mrs Rosenberg's shriek of horror split the sultry air behind them.

"I don't know what's got into you!" bemoaned Mitzi's mother.

"Look, darling," the serious expression on her father's face caused Mitzi no end of amusement. "Your mother and I were wondering ... are you taking drugs?" Mitzi laughed in an unearthly, lascivious manner. There was something familiar about that laugh, but Mitzi's mother couldn't quite place it.

"The blood tests were negative," Doctor Warner told Mitzi's parents. Of course, your daughter might have taken a drug that metabolised quickly out of her body, but the lab certainly didn't find any sign of any of the more common substances. You know, it's not infrequent for young women of Mitzi's age to have psychological problems. I have a friend who's an excellent psychologist. I can put you in touch with him if you like."

"It's nothing more than a healthy appetite for life," Dr Friedmann told Mitzi's parents, winking at the girl when they weren't looking. Mitzi winked back, uncrossing and re-crossing her legs in a manner worthy of a sleazy Hollywood movie, and giving her psychologist a tantalising flash that reminded him of all the fun they'd had in their two months of £220 per hour therapy sessions. "But I'll be happy to go on working with Mitzi … and I can give you a big discount."

"That won't be necessary, Doctor," said Mitzi's father. "Thank you all the same."

Mitzi's parents watched in horror as their only child flirted outrageously with all their male friends – and their sons, brothers, cousins and fathers. They stopped inviting men to the house, and succeeded admirably in beating Mitzi to the door or distracting her when the postman rang. But then disaster struck.

With everything that was going on, Mitzi's mother had totally forgotten that she'd booked the gardener for his monthly visit. She and Mitzi's father had gone out to run some errands and got back to find raunchy music blasting from Mitzi's bedroom. They hurried upstairs, with a growing feeling of unease, and found the perplexed, but delighted gardener tied to a chair wearing nothing but his boxer shorts and being given a lap dance by their daughter who was proudly sporting her edible undies. Needless to say, this was not a sight that any parent should be forced to endure, and the poor gardener was promptly untied and given his marching orders. They couldn't lock her in the house, as she was an adult, but Mitzi's parents knew that they had to act fast. They had to save their daughter before she went back to college, where she would be beyond their control and where there was no telling what kind of trouble she'd get herself into.

"I know it sounds crazy," Mitzi's mother told her husband, "but that's not my daughter – that's not Mitzi." But it wasn't until Mitzi dyed her hair a particularly offensive shade of peroxide blonde, and the unmistakable family resemblance glared her defiantly in the face, that Mitzi's mother realised the full implication of what she'd started to suspect on a subconscious level.

"I think a *dybbuk* has entered my daughter," Mitzi's mother told the Rabbi.

"Nonsense!" he replied. But his scepticism vanished as Mitzi – who'd been standing quietly behind her mother – lifted up her top and gave the holy man a quick flash of her bare breasts.

"It's my late sister," Mitzi's mother continued, thankfully unaware of her child's actions behind her back. "She was a prolific whore from the day she turned sixteen to the day she got hit by a truck... I suppose there's one in every family."

So it was that with considerable hesitation the Rabbi consented to perform a banishing ritual. For many days he negotiated with the spirit of Mitzi's aunt to depart the young woman's body before getting her into no end of trouble. The *dybbuk* said that it would leave only if the Rabbi performed lewd acts with the girl, and it took all of the Rabbi's strength of character to push from his mind the images that the misguided spirit planted within it.

The holy man bored her to tears. Sometimes his droning voice and inane arguments wearied her so much that she actually thought about leaving her beautiful fleshy home just to avoid listening to him a moment longer. But there was no way she was going to relinquish her last chance at happiness.

The Rabbi did everything in his power to persuade Mitzi's aunt to leave the innocent girl and move on. But all his attempts came to naught. And then an extraordinary opportunity presented itself.

"Rabbi, we need your help." The recently wed couple stood before him; the young man sweating and embarrassed, his wife visibly distressed. "All we want is to live a good life in the eyes of God," the young man said.

"And to bear children in his image," added the woman. Her pale cheeks were tinged scarlet with shame, and when she briefly lifted her eyes from the floor, the Rabbi saw that there were tears in them.

"But, you see Rabbi," the man carried on, "my wife just can't bear when I touch her."

"It's not you; it's me," the young woman interjected in her husband's defence.

"I am gentle and I try to give her pleasure…"

"But, I just can't, Rabbi … even the very thought of it makes me sick."

The Rabbi couldn't sleep that night. He tossed and turned, and scanned his memory of *halakhah*, trying to find the right path for all his supplicants. And then it came to him: he would bake two proverbial *challot* in one pan! If he couldn't persuade the dirty *dybbuk* to move on to the next plane of existence, then perhaps he could talk it into moving to a more suitable home.

And so, not only was Mitzi liberated from the burden of unwanted wantonness, but the troubled couple became eternally indebted to the Rabbi – for many fine children, and countless nights, mornings, and even lunchtimes of the most satisfactory wedded bliss.

And Mitzi's aunt had no complaints.

UNDERBELLY

It had taken weeks to get a doctor's appointment, then months to persuade her general practitioner to refer her to a specialist, more months to get the hospital appointment with the specialist, more weeks for the results of the undignified and painful tests to which she was subjected to be analysed, another week for the test results to get back to her GP, and a few more days for Anna's GP to call her in and say that there was nothing they could do – perhaps if they'd caught it a couple of months sooner it wouldn't have spread from her cervix to the rest of her abdomen, from where it was already on its way through her lymph system to her entire body.

Anna struggled to find a position in which she could survive the night, survive the next five minutes, survive the next few seconds. She tried curling up into a ball; she tried lying on her back with her knees bent. She started thrashing about on the bed in pain and fell onto the floor, where she started to crawl towards the front door. Sweat poured down her face, her entire body fired up by the pain in her underbelly.

Anna reached the door and grabbed hold of the handle, pulling herself up. She left her bedsit and stumbled blindly along the corridors of the horrible old building. It had once been a Victorian school or lunatic asylum – Anna didn't know which and at this point in time she didn't care. She reached the fire door leading out onto the staircase and, clutching the handrail, she stumbled downstairs, not knowing what she was doing or where she was going. She kept going down as far as she could. She reached the ground floor, but kept going downwards until she could go no further. She stopped for a moment and looked around, surprised to find herself in the basement. Then a particularly violent wave of pain hit her and she fell to her knees, retching.

After a couple of minutes Anna got up shakily, and walked ahead – into the dark winding corridors of the building. She needed to keep moving forward, moving into the darkness. Maybe if she disappeared into the darkness, the pain would disappear too. Anna had never been adventurous by nature, but, delirious with pain, she stumbled on into a place she would not have had the slightest urge to go near had she been in her right mind. Finally she found herself in the farthest corner of the basement – there really was nowhere else to go. Anna clawed at the brick wall in despair and a fresh wave of tears stained her face as she cried out loud into the night. After a long while she turned to go and her foot caught on something. She fell heavily, and for the briefest second it appeared that the sharp pain in her hands and knees would silence the pain in her belly, but no – it seemed that nothing could do that. And there it was – once dull and throbbing, once sharp as glass.

Anna felt around in the darkness for what had tripped her up. It was a large metal ring. She tried to pick it up, but found that it was attached – to what turned out to be a trapdoor in the basement floor. Anna worked out the perimeter of the trapdoor, and moved to one side of it. Then, using all her strength, she pulled at the ring. Eventually the door shifted and came loose. There was just enough light for Anna to make out wooden steps leading into the blackness. Her thoughts started to race in a bid to work out what might be down there – if the muddled images and disconnected flashes that fired in Anna's pain-addled brain could be described as thoughts. Not knowing why or how, she descended into what appeared to be a cellar. She had almost made it down when the pain increased again to an unbearable pitch, causing her to cry out and fall from the final step to the damp ground beneath, where she crawled a metre or so, then curled up into a ball and lay clutching her abdomen.

When Anna finally stopped crying, she listened to the beating of her own heart. But then she thought she heard something else – far too close for comfort – the sound of something moving in the dark. Anna lay as still as she could and willed her heart to stop beating so loudly. The sound came again. *Rats*, she thought. But then she heard what sounded like a cross between a growl and a squeal – two-toned – low and guttural, yet at the same time high and penetrating. It was like no sound she had ever heard, and, even though she had wished for death a thousand times in the past weeks, Anna suddenly feared for her life.

The chilling feral sound came again. Before the cancer took over her life, Anna had enjoyed watching nature programmes, and she was familiar with the sounds made by even the strangest animals living in the remotest places on earth. But that mewling, growling sound didn't come from any animal on earth that Anna could think of. The movement and the growl came again, and Anna started backing towards the steps leading out of the cellar. She had almost reached the bottom one when a guttural shriek froze the blood in her veins, causing every hair on her body to stand on end. She felt a rush of air as something hurled itself at her at unnatural speed, hitting her side hard enough to spin her round. The force of the impact threw her across the cellar, and she screamed as something sharp pierced her belly. Then she was lying against the cellar wall, paralysed with fear, the creature that had attacked her sitting on her, what she assumed to be its fangs buried in her abdomen.

Anna's eyes had grown accustomed to the dark and she could see the thing that was on top of her, almost crushing the breath out of her. It had short, black, course fur, rather like that of a tarantula, it was muscular like a Rottweiler, and almost round in shape. Its appearance reminded Anna of the vile creatures in the Hieronymus Bosch paintings she had seen in the Louvre as an art student.

As Anna prepared for death, the strangest thing happened. The creature evidently still had its fangs – rather like those of a giant spider – embedded in her abdomen, but Anna realised that not only did she no longer feel the sharp pain from the fangs, but for the first time in weeks the pain in her belly was bearable. In fact, the pain in her belly was slowly draining away – fading away to nothing. Anna stared down her body at the thing that she assumed was feeding on her, wondering whether it had injected her with some kind of anaesthetising substance – like a mosquito or a vampire bat – so that it could drain all the life out of her without her even being aware. If that was the case, then so be it; her only regret being that her corpse would rot down here, in the dark, with no one knowing what had happened to her, and no trace of her left – not even a tombstone to state that she, Anna Weedon, had ever lived at all. It would be as though she never even existed, never walked the earth for thirty-nine years. But she could live with that – or die with that – as long as there was no more pain.

As Anna gave herself up completely to the creature, it suddenly withdrew its fangs from her abdomen and looked at her. Its slanted red eyes glowed with an unfathomable malevolence. Those eyes were more human than animal, and yet they were neither. They bored into Anna's mind, seeing every dark thought she'd ever had, every sin she'd ever committed, every crime she'd ever contemplated. Those eyes spoke of places darker and more horrifying than anything Anna could imagine – anything, that is, except her pain.

"Thank you," Anna managed to utter as the creature shifted slightly, allowing her to breathe more easily. It bared its massive, long, bone-coloured, slightly curved fangs at Anna in what could have been a grin. "Are you going to eat me now?" Anna asked, calm and strangely clear-headed now that the pain was gone.

"Not you."

Despite her resignation to whatever fate the creature had in store for her, Anna jolted in fear as the unspoken voice rang in her ears. She had never heard a voice like that before – loud and jarring, while at the same time sounding as if it came from a million miles away – from the bottom of hell itself. She stared at the creature, but its hideous grinning mouth hadn't uttered those words. "I don't want *you*," the voice in Anna's mind continued. "You're already being eaten – from the inside out. Why would I want to eat *you*?"

"Then why did you inject the venom into me ... the anaesthetic ... whatever it was?" asked Anna.

"I didn't inject anything into you. I just took the pain away."

"Thank you ... but why?" Anna gazed into the red all-knowing, all-seeing eyes. She knew from those eyes that the creature must be very old, extremely wise, and exceedingly malign.

"You disturbed me. I was asleep for a long time and you woke me. I knew I couldn't eat you – I could smell your disease a mile away. But I'm very hungry and you have to feed me. I took the pain away so you can bring me others,"

"Others...? You mean people?"

"Yes."

"I can't bring you people."

"You have to." The creature hissed at Anna through its fangs and increased the pressure on her abdomen, making it hard for her to breathe.

"I can't."

"You will."

"I'm very grateful that you made the pain go away," gasped Anna, "but I can't bring you people to eat. I wouldn't even know how to, even if I wanted to."

"You'll work it out, once the pain is back."

Just then, that familiar twinge in her abdomen and Anna cried out as the pain came flooding back into her body.

"No, please!"

"Very well," said the voice in Anna's head, and she breathed a sigh of relief as the pain dissipated. "But I need to eat. You will bring me someone tomorrow night or the pain will be back and it will be worse than ever."

"Okay," Anna promised.

Then, as quickly as it had assaulted her, the creature leapt off her and merged with the shadows in the cellar. In the instant before it disappeared from sight, Anna noticed that it had two powerful muscular hind legs, two long ungainly arms that it used to walk on some of the time, leaning on its knuckles – rather like an ape – and two membranous wings that were folded along its sides, which it also occasionally used for support while walking – rather like a bat. Anna got up slowly and headed up the steps out of the cellar, eventually making her way back to her bedsit. The first light of dawn was breaking over the horizon and the dawn chorus was raising hell outside Anna's tiny window.

Anna sat on her bed for a long time, wondering if she had imagined the whole thing, but the glorious lack of pain in her belly dispelled any doubts that there really had been a foul-smelling hideous demon in the cellar, which had bitten her and taken her pain away. And told her to bring it people to eat. Yeah, right... Wasn't it more likely that the whole thing had been a nightmare – the creature, the pain, the hospital visits, the cancer? Wasn't it more likely that she'd fallen asleep and dreamt the last few unbearable months in several minutes of cruel REM sleep, her mind summing up her greatest fears and conjuring them up in the night to torment her? If only that were true...

Anna looked around the room and noticed how dusty it was, how dirty. She looked into a mirror and winced, as a hundred-year-old woman with a sickly complexion, dark rings under her eyes and long strands of greasy hair looked back at her. *Christ.* She spent the rest of the morning cleaning the bedsit, having a bath, washing her hair and putting on make-up. She was surprised at how good she felt despite having had no sleep whatsoever. She looked in the mirror again and, satisfied that she looked thirty-nine once more, she got dressed and went out in search of food. She felt hungry without simultaneously feeling sick for the first time in months, and, as she walked to her local Morrison's for lunch and supplies, she smiled as men eyed her up in the street – admiring her ample breasts and long legs.

Anna spent the afternoon wandering around the local park, soaking up the sunshine, delighting in life and lack of pain. For a moment she even thought about phoning Frank – the love of her life, the man she had spent seven wonderful months with until the growing pain and the constant hospital visits and waiting – for referrals, for appointments, for results – had dampened her sunny disposition, making her moody, grumpy and needy. Added to that the fact that Anna's inability to get work during the recession had shrunk her bank account to nothing, and Frank had evaporated like the last breath of a dying man. His departure had left Anna heartbroken and with no desire to live, the cancer seizing this great opportunity to attack her grief-weakened body with extra vigour and speed. But it would take a lot more than Anna's undying love, and desire to see him, to bring Frank back.

As night fell, Anna remembered the creature's words and started to fear that the pain would return. She watched television for a while, but couldn't concentrate on anything, and decided to go to bed as normal. She was tired after a full day of cleaning, shopping, walking, and the previous night's lack of sleep started to take its toll. She dozed off at around eleven pm, thinking that perhaps she would be okay.

At midnight, Anna awoke screaming. The pain in her abdomen was like being stabbed over and over, as if a medieval executioner were thrusting a blunt saw into her underbelly and twisting it slowly, only to pull it out again, and stab her a few more times. Anna grabbed the bottle of painkillers by her bed and thrust a couple of pills into her mouth, gagging as she tried to swallow them without water. She staggered to the kitchen and turned on the cold water tap, not waiting for it to run for a while, but drinking the water lukewarm and cloudy – the liquid splashing over her face and chest.

It would take time for the pills to start working. Anna knew from experience that lying down wouldn't help, that sitting wouldn't help, so she staggered around the bedsit, bumping into the walls, knocking things over, hoping that the movement would accelerate her heartbeat and speed the drugs through her bloodstream, making them work quicker. After five minutes she couldn't wait any longer – she would take more pills, even if it killed her, which might, in any case, be for the best. She got a handful out of the bottle and swallowed them down with water, this time from a glass, but her body started to spasm violently and she retched, bringing up the whole lot – drugs, water and all.

The pain in her abdomen was like a spiky metal ball thumping her over and over, doubling her up and making her curse God, curse herself, the world and everyone in it. Suddenly she was urinating all over herself – the pain such that all control over her pelvic muscles was gone. Howling and humiliated, Anna ran for the door, for the stairs, for the basement, for the cellar, for the abomination that she prayed to the Devil was waiting for her in the darkness.

Anna slid down the cellar steps on her behind and crawled blindly forward into the darkness. Fear mixed with relief as she heard a growl-squeal ahead of her, and the familiar gust of displaced air hit her a split second before she was thrown backwards, the creature crushing the breath out of her with its heavy, compact body.

"Where's my food?"

"Please," Anna begged, "Make it go away."

"Where's my food?"

"I hurt."

"How do you think I feel? I haven't eaten for eighty years."

"Make it go away."

"Will you bring me food?"

"Yes. I swear," Anna gasped under the weight of the creature on top of her. "I swear on my mother's grave. Just make it go away." The familiar short sharp stabbing pain as the fangs sank into her abdomen, and then the sweet gentle relief as the pain subsided and disappeared. "Thank you."

The creature glared at Anna furiously. "You have one hour to bring me food or it will be back and it will stay until you die screaming."

"Two hours," bargained Anna, her brain suddenly crystal clear and computing ways of bringing it food. She remembered the way men had looked at her in the street on her way to the supermarket. In the anonymity of darkness men like that would be even more willing to act upon their sordid impulses with a complete stranger.

"Two hours," agreed the creature, reading Anna's every thought and emotion, and grinning at the woman with its bone-coloured fangs. The cancer may take her body, but the creature would have her soul – and that was far more satisfying.

"Blondie!" The man was drunk and horny. He'd been drinking in the pub all evening with his mates, but had popped out for a quick smoke. When he saw the big-titted blonde in the short skirt walking past, he thought that Christmas had come early. Any woman with legs like that was obviously gagging for it, and he wasn't going to take no for an answer. He looked around the street – it was empty apart from him and the girl. He looked back into the pub – no one was paying any attention to him, the Chelsea-Manchester United match keeping all eyes glued firmly to the television screen on the wall. "Hey, blondie!"

Anna instinctively ignored the man and was about to walk past, when he grabbed her arm.

"Hey darling," the man slurred in Anna's ear, "I been waiting for you."

"Have you?" asked Anna, her heart pounding with fear. All her damaged insides needed now was to get raped by this large brute.

"We're gonna have some fun, baby," the man told Anna, pulling her away from the pub. "I know this great alley just round the corner – very romantic."

"I know somewhere even better," Anna mustered all her courage to steady her voice.

"Oh yeah? Where's that?"

"My place," Anna told him. The man paused for a moment, looking doubtful.

"Yeah?"

"Yeah. It's just round the corner."

"You're having me on."

"No, I'm not." The man still had a strong grip on Anna's right arm, so she used her left hand to fondle his genitals.

"Let's do it right here." Anna winced as the man thrust his hand between her legs.

"I thought you were a romantic," she said, trying to push his hand away.

"Oh I am. A right romantic – that's me."

"Well, let's go back to my place then, and make a night of it." Anna tried to move off in the direction of her street. The man threw a glance over his shoulder toward the pub, then shrugged and let himself be led back to Anna's building.

"Where we going?" the man asked, making another attempt to pull Anna's top off as they walked through the basement.

"Be patient. We're nearly there." Anna tried to keep the man's rough hands off her as she led him towards the cellar.

"Right, that's far enough, I'm having you right here."

"Wait! It's just there." Anna pointed to the corner of the basement.

"What is?"

"The entrance to the cellar."

"I'm not going in any cellar, you stupid bitch." The man threw Anna on the floor.

"Wait. It's really cosy down there. Really nice, you'll see."
Anna backed away from the man on her backside, scraping
herself on the basement floor. "It's just there – look!"

"I don't see nothing."

"There on the floor. You see the ring?" The man peered into
the shadows. "You just need to pull it up and there are steps
leading down. It's really nice down there. Like a secret love den.
There's a mattress, and beer, and everything,"

"You're talking shit."

"Just look!"

The man's curiosity got the better of him. He pulled up the
trapdoor and peered down into the gloom.

"I don't see anything,"

"Once we get down, I'll switch on the light."

"You want to lock me in down there!"

"No, I don't." The man was getting angry and Anna was
getting very frightened. "I'll go down first, okay? Look, I'm
going down first."

Anna bolted down the steps and the man followed cautiously.
She was going to pay for bringing him down here. He had
planned to treat her nice, but now he was going to do her hard
and rough for dragging him all the way down into this stinking
damp place.

The man descended the steps slowly, backwards, like a ladder.

"So where's the light switch?" he demanded, and the next
thing he knew – there was a snarling, howling sound and
something struck him in the chest. He was thrown backwards,
his chest, neck, stomach, face exploding in blood and chunks of
flesh as fangs and claws moved over him and inside him at
lightning speed. He was dead before he hit the cellar floor.

Anna screamed as blood splattered all around her. She hid
behind the cellar steps and whimpered as the snarling, tearing
sounds continued. As her eyes grew accustomed to the dark, she
could see the creature devouring the man – chunk by chunk.
Anna threw up, then wiped her mouth and cried. The man had
been a sleaze, but he hadn't deserved this: he was being eaten

like a piece of steak, and she was responsible. Anna cried for the man, she cried for any family he might have left behind and she cried for her immortal soul. But after a while, she wiped her eyes and found herself pondering how it was that the creature could eat the entire man in one sitting. It hadn't just been eating the man's flesh; it had been crunching up his bones with logic-defying ease and swallowing those as well. There was almost nothing left of the man, except the tattered remains of his clothes, and Anna wondered why the fiend's stomach didn't burst. Her repulsion and guilt turned to a morbid curiosity, and she peered out from behind the steps, watching the black furry winged thing feed. It was quite impressive really – the thing was one efficient eating machine. Anna wondered whether it had an extending stomach, her mind conjuring up images from *The Little Prince*, which her grandmother had read to her when she was little, and in which she remembered seeing a picture of what looked like a hat, but was actually meant to be a snake that had swallowed an elephant.

As Anna's mind drifted back to her childhood, the creature finished its feast and looked through the cellar steps at the woman. Anna noticed its blazing red eyes and cowered back in fear, but then remembered that it wasn't going to eat her. The fiend looked into Anna for a long while, then turned away and moved off languidly into the shadows.

"By midnight tomorrow," the distant, deafening voice reverberated through Anna's mind, and then the monstrosity was gone. Anna took a last look at the bloodstained rags lying on the cellar floor and hurried back to her bedsit.

Anna woke up late after the previous night's horrors, and lay in bed thinking about Frank. She had given every single atom of her being over to loving him. Her tutor at university had told her – after she had been dumped by her first love – that she shouldn't give all of herself away to a man; that she should always hold a little bit back for herself, so as not to give another human being the power to destroy her completely if things went wrong. She'd followed her tutor's advice throughout all her subsequent relationships, but everything changed when she met Frank. She was so convinced that he was her soul mate and that they would stay together forever, that she forgot her tutor's words. She had let herself go for the first time since she was eighteen, and allowed herself to fall in love completely – catering to Frank's every whim; giving him love, sex, money and everything he asked for. But when she had asked for more than the one night a week he was willing to give her, he had turned on her, comparing her to his ex and telling her that he didn't need 'any of that emotional stuff.' The final straw had come when Anna didn't have any more money to 'lend' him. The loans, which added up to a couple of thousand pounds over seven months – were ones that Anna never expected to get back, and Frank had no complaints about that. Anna realised how ridiculously one-sided their relationship had been, but she didn't care. Now that the pain no longer filled her entire world, she felt a large gap in her life – a gap that only Frank could fill.

"Hello?" Anna's blood pressure shot up as she heard Frank's voice on the other end of the phone. Her heart was pounding, and she could feel herself getting light-headed.

"Frank, it's Anna."

There was a long pause at the other end, then Frank said, "I thought you told me you were dying."

"I am," said Anna, fighting back the tears that were welling up in her eyes – tears not about her imminent death, but about the cold tone in Frank's voice that she had come to dread in their last weeks together. "But I'm feeling better at the moment and I was hoping you could come over."

"I'm working,"

"After work, then."

"Look, it's over, Anna. We're not together anymore."

"I know, it's just that I…"

"It's just that you what?"

"I…" Anna felt herself drowning. Like that time when Frank said he couldn't handle how needy and emotional she was, and that he couldn't be with her anymore. She looked around for a straw to grasp before the water closed over her head. "I've won the lottery," she blurted out, regretting her words the moment they were out.

"You what?"

She could tell he wasn't buying it – he could see right through her ridiculous lie. Anna panicked and dug herself in deeper. "Not millions or anything. Just three hundred and eighty thousand. You know, five balls and the bonus ball."

Silence at the other end. Then, "You're kidding!"

"No, I'm not. I really won it. Ironic, isn't it – winning the lottery when I'm about to die."

"I can't believe it!" Frank couldn't believe he hadn't stayed with the needy, whining bitch. It would have been worth it. Three hundred and eighty thousand. He could have left his crappy dead-end job and become a fulltime writer. Maybe there was still time... "That's fantastic, baby!" he told Anna.

"It's true." Anna had always loved it when he called her 'baby'. "That's why I'm calling, actually."

"I'm so happy for you, baby!"

"Yeah, well. You know, I'm not going to spend all of it and I've been thinking that, well, if I let you have some of it – most of it – you could give up your job like you wanted and become a fulltime writer."

"I couldn't take your money, baby."

"I've got no one else to leave it to. It's not like I've got any children, or any brothers and sisters. My parents are dead, and I never liked my cousins, so I just thought..."

"Baby, I can't believe you thought of me. I don't know what to say. I mean... I couldn't take your money, but maybe if I could borrow some – just until I sell my first novel..."

"Yeah, well, maybe you could come over tonight?"

"Sure, I can come over. What time were you thinking?"

"As soon as you can after work. I can cook some dinner?"

"Sure. That'll be great." The bitch couldn't cook for shit, but he'd eat dog turd if it meant he could get his hands on three hundred and eighty thousand. "I'll get to yours for about half six."

"Great," said Anna. "I've missed you," she added tentatively.

"I've missed you too," echoed Frank, without much conviction. Anna had a strong urge to say, 'Well, you could have called me anytime', but she refrained. She hung up the phone and felt happy for a few moments, but then the reality of the situation hit her and the panic returned. She would put on some really sexy, feminine clothes and cook a nice dinner, she would be cheerful and she wouldn't talk about her illness. Perhaps when Frank spent some time with her, perhaps when they made love and he saw that things could be back to how they used to be, he would forget about the money and forgive her for making it all up – he would understand that she'd done it because she loved him and wanted to see him. Perhaps... But who was she really kidding?

Frank arrived, looking every bit as sexy as when Anna first laid eyes on him. He froze when Anna went to hug him, shattering any hope she might have had about them getting back together. Dinner was awkward: Anna waiting on Frank, nervous about her cooking, Frank forcing himself to be polite and not to be the first to mention the lottery money. When they had finished dessert, Anna leaned over and tried to kiss him, but Frank pulled away.

"Cancer isn't contagious, you know," Anna told him.

"Look, Anna, I really appreciate you helping me out with the money..."

"Frank, there's something I have to tell you..."

"What is it?" There was a long silence as Anna thought frantically whether to tell him or not. "Well?"

"There is no money."

"What?"

"I really wanted to see you..."

"What do you mean there is no money?"

"I'm sorry. I really wanted to see you..."

"So you pretended to win the lottery?"

"I'm sorry."

"You stupid fucking bitch! You made me leave Monica and come all the way over here..."

"What do you mean, leave Monica?" Anna suddenly felt sick.
"We were supposed to go out to dinner tonight..."

"You're back with your ex?"

"I'm not *back* with her, Anna. I've always been with her."
The room spun and Anna had to hold onto the table.

"But when we met, you said you'd split up with her six months
earlier."

"Yeah well, I didn't think you'd sleep with me if I told you the
truth."

"So all the time we were together you were living with
Monica?"

"Oh, come on, Anna; don't try to tell me you didn't know."

"How could I possibly have known?"

"I never had you over at my place; I hardly ever stayed the
night at yours." The pathetic look on Anna's face was really
winding Frank up. "For God's sake, Anna, don't tell me you're
that fucking naive?"

"So our whole relationship was a lie?" Anna could hear her
voice cracking up, but there was absolutely no way she was
going to cry in front of Frank again.

"Look, I'm not here to discuss our non-existent relationship. It
was over ages ago. If there's no money, then I'm going." Frank
got up to leave.

"Wait!" The change in Anna's tone stopped Frank in his
tracks. "There is money. You can have it. But you have to help
me get it out. It's in the basement."

"What?" Frank looked at Anna and she searched his eyes for
the slightest hint of the man she thought had loved her. She saw
only a mixture of incredulity, contempt and greed.

"It's not safe in here. There's all sorts of people going up and
down the corridor, and my flat isn't very secure. One kick and
they're through the door. So I hid it in the basement."

"You hid three hundred and eighty thousand pounds in the
basement?"

"It's only three hundred thousand. I'm using the rest to get
proper healthcare."

"Whatever... Are you having me on?"

169

"Frank, it's okay that you're still with Monica. Maybe we could still..."

"For God's sake, Anna!"

Anna raised her hand to stem Frank's anger.

"Okay. Let's go get the money."

"Can't you just bring it up and I'll wait here?" If anyone was dumb enough to keep three hundred thousand pounds in a damp rodent-infested basement – if the money even existed – it was Anna, but he didn't fancy creeping around in the dark, looking for it.

"It's heavy – there's quite a lot of it. It's best if we go together."

"Alright," sighed Frank. "Let's go."

As he watched Anna descending the stairs into the cellar, Frank was not happy. He wondered whether there was in fact any money, he wondered whether Anna even had cancer; he had often wondered whether she had made the cancer up just to pressure him into spending more time with her. He was tempted to turn around and walk away, but even the slimmest chance of three hundred thousand pounds was something you didn't just walk away from.

Anna paused at the top of the steps and looked back at Frank, searching his face in the darkness one last time. Nothing there – only impatience, wariness and annoyance. Anna continued down the steps, the tears she'd been holding back finally breaking out and trickling down her face.

Anna lay whimpering in the corner, her eyes closed until the creature finished feeding. Frank hadn't even had time to cry out, but Anna heard the tearing, slurping, crunching sounds despite clamping her hands over her ears. When the sounds ceased and Anna opened her eyes, the creature was gone. Anna threw up her dinner, returned to her bedsit and cried herself to sleep.

Anna was still grieving over Frank when the time came to provide the creature's next meal. She found that most of her former friends – friends who had suddenly become very busy when Anna's money ran out and even busier when she got sick – were more than willing to visit her at short notice when she told them about her lottery win. On nights when nobody wanted to come over, she went out and brought back men.

One night she was watching the thing feed on a married stockbroker called George, when she found herself admiring its thick black fur and the way the scant light falling into the cellar penetrated its extraordinary membranous wings. She wondered if it could actually fly. As it finished feeding and turned to go, Anna called out to it.

"Wait!"

The bloated fiend turned back and gazed at Anna, mild interest in its slanted red eyes, its fangs bared in what looked to Anna like a grin.

"You feed so fast," Anna said to it. "I mean, you kill so fast... I'll bring you someone tomorrow night. I was wondering if you could ... kill that person ... slowly?"

The creature contemplated the woman before him for a few moments. A hollow, sinister laugh reverberated in Anna's ears.

"Very well," the thing said finally, its mouth never moving as it spoke. "I'll eat your doctor slowly."

"How did you know...?"

"I can see inside you."

Anna's GP refused to speak to her and, after many phone calls and much pestering of the receptionist, when he did finally talk to her, he refused to come.

"I don't make house calls," he told her.

"But I'm in pain, Doctor," pleaded Anna, "I'm scared. Please, I'm too sick to leave the house today, and my painkillers have run out."

"If you feel so bad, you should call an ambulance."

"Please, Doctor. I've been your patient for fifteen years. Please, I need you... I can make it worth your while."

"Don't be stupid, Ms Weedon. The NHS pays my wages, and I don't make house calls."

"I didn't mean to offend you, Doctor. It's just that I won the lottery recently, and I don't have anyone to leave the money to. And you've been my doctor for fifteen years. I thought you could do with the money – perhaps you could expand your private practice. And I really need you to come over tonight. Please."

"You won the lottery?"

"Yes, Doctor, and I would really like to leave you the money when I die – which, as you know, won't be long now."

"Well, I guess I could make an exception. After all, you *are* an exceptional patient, and I *have* been your doctor for fifteen years…"

It had been hard getting her GP to come down to the basement, but it had been worth it. The creature was true to its word and killed the doctor slowly, holding him down while it ate him piece by piece, making sure the man could see and hear his own flesh being chewed and swallowed.

Anna's doctor screamed to her to save him.

"Help me! Get it off!"

"*You* should have helped *me*, the first time I came to you with bleeding and abdominal pain," Anna screamed back at him.

"Please, help me!"

"No!"

The doctor continued to scream and struggle, but the creature held him firm, and his movements weakened as exhaustion, blood loss and excruciating pain sapped his strength. Through the darkness and the tears that were streaming down his face, he thought he could see Anna smiling.

"Why?" he gurgled at her, blood spewing from his mouth.

"Because it takes away my pain, which is more than you ever bothered to do!"

Despite the creature's best efforts to keep him alive as long as possible, after half an hour of being eaten, the doctor's heart finally gave out and stopped. Five minutes later, there was no trace of him left, apart from some bloody, tattered rags. The creature turned to go, but Anna called it back.

"Wait!"

The monstrosity turned back and the two of them eyed each other for a long while.

"May I touch you?" Anna finally asked.

"Why do you want to touch me?"

"You're my only friend."

The creature laughed – that distant, hollow, grating laugh that scared Anna, even as the creature itself no longer scared her – well, not as much as it used to.

"You fed me all your other friends," the creature grinned with its bony, bloody fangs.

"They weren't my friends. Not really. They never did anything for me. Not like you."

"Touch me then." The creature found the woman amusing. It was always entertaining to watch how fast humans gave away their immortal souls – and all their nearest and dearest – to get what they wanted: money, success, sex, longer life, an end to pain. It was enough to look inside them, see what they wanted the most, and once you offered it to them, they just rolled over for you.

Anna crawled uncertainly over to the creature and reached out a trembling hand. When she found that the fiend didn't bite it off, she gently touched its black fur. Anna was amazed to find that its fur was quite soft – not hard and bristly as she had thought. As she stroked the monster's fur, it narrowed its red eyes – rather like a cat – and after a while it started to purr-mewl. Under its fur, the creature's muscular body was round and firm. Exhaustion overcame Anna; she leant her head against the creature and fell asleep.

In the early hours of the morning, the cold woke Anna up. She was lying on the damp floor of the cellar alone; the creature was gone.

The next day, a policeman and policewoman came round to Anna's flat and asked whether she had seen her doctor the previous day – he had not returned home last night and had not turned up to work in the morning. His last appointment had been Anna's house call.

Anna said that he had been with her for about ten minutes, and then left.

"What was the exact purpose of his visit?" The policeman tried to make himself comfortable on the small sofa.

"He prescribed me some painkillers."

"Can we see the prescription, please?"

Anna's heart started to pound, and she had to think fast.

"I don't have the prescription anymore," she said. "I already bought the medicine."

"Can we see the medicine, please," said the policeman.

"Of course." Anna went to the bathroom and started looking for an old bottle of pills. The GP had been so keen to discuss the money that the two of them had forgotten all about the painkillers that Anna had said she needed. She finally found a bottle half filled with pills and brought it in.

"That's only half full." The policeman took the bottle from Anna, and studied it closely. "And it was issued a month ago."

"Oh," Anna was starting to panic. "I didn't notice, I'm sorry – I'm not very well. I have cancer, you know. Perhaps you can help me find the right bottle."

"That won't be necessary." The policeman smiled sympathetically. The policewoman also smiled, but her smile didn't reach her eyes.

Barely a few days had passed, and the police were back, questioning Anna about her friend Teresa.

"We understand from her husband, that she came to see you last week."

"No, she didn't." Anna was feeling sick again. "I mean, she was meant to come and see me, but she never showed up."

"So what did you do when she didn't show up?" asked the policewoman. "Did you call her house?"

Anna had the distinct feeling that both the policewoman and the policeman knew the answer to that already.

Underbelly

"No, I didn't," Anna told them. "I didn't do anything. I mean, Teresa often told me that she would be coming round, and then I wouldn't hear from her for six months. I didn't think anything had happened to her."

"Her husband said that you'd won the lottery and that you wanted to give her some of your money. Is this true?"

"No, it's not true."

"No, you didn't win the lottery, or no, you didn't tell Mrs Trent that you'd won the lottery."

"Neither."

"Then why would Mr Trent say such a thing?"

"I don't know."

"I think you told Mrs Trent that you'd won the lottery and that you'd give her the money, and when she came here and found that there was no money, the two of you had an argument and something happened."

"Like what?"

"Like maybe you killed her."

"What! How can you say that? I wouldn't kill anyone. I've got cancer, you know."

"Yes, we know."

"I told you, Teresa wasn't even here."

"Well, two of your neighbours told us they saw a woman matching Mrs Trent's description entering the building."

"Well, she wasn't here."

The policewoman sat back, finished for the moment. Her colleague took over.

"Do you mind if we have a look around?" he asked. Anna shook her head. They found nothing.

"We'll be back," they told Anna on their way out. And they were – a few days later.

This time the two police officers were armed with a list of missing people – all linked by the fact that they knew Anna – and more eyewitness testimony: concerning men entering the building with a woman who matched Anna's description. Anna co-operated and gave them a full statement, under threat of

175

having to do so at the police station. A further search of her bedsit revealed nothing, but Anna was sure that they were watching the entrance to her building.

That evening she went down to see the creature, empty-handed.

"I can't feed you for a while," she tried to explain. "The police are watching the building. I can't bring anyone here."

"I need to eat," the creature's voice resounded in Anna's ears, and the fiend's eyes blazed at Anna angrily.

"I can't bring anyone."

"If you don't feed me, the pain will return."

Anna felt that familiar twinge in her abdomen. She hadn't felt it for weeks now, and she doubled over, clutching her underbelly and crying out.

"Stop! Please stop! I thought you were my friend." It would be a lie to say that the fiend's betrayal of their 'friendship' hurt almost as much as Anna's abdomen, but it hurt nonetheless.

"I *am* your friend," the creature told Anna. The pain subsided, but Anna was left reeling and scared. "You will bring me someone tonight and I will continue to be your friend."

Anna found the young Polish man sitting on a bench in the local park, drinking a can of beer. By the look of the grass around the bench, he had drunk more than one already. His English was poor, he had obviously not been in London long, and was homesick and lonely. Anna told him that her boyfriend had dumped her and she needed someone to walk her home, as she didn't like walking home on her own in the dark. She didn't know if the young man understood what she was saying, but he certainly seemed keen enough to follow her home, and drunk enough to accompany her to the cellar.

As Anna led the man down the steps, she had a change of heart. He had done nothing wrong: he hadn't betrayed her, he hadn't tried to grope her, judging by the lack of ring on his ring finger he wasn't hoping to cheat on his wife with her. All he had done was walk her home and smile at her in a tipsy, perplexed kind of way. Anna stopped abruptly on the steps and was about to tell the man to go back up, that this had all been a mistake, but just then bright lights appeared behind them, followed by running footsteps and shouting.

"Police! Freeze!"

Anna screamed and tried to run down the remaining steps, but slipped and fell. Her head hit something hard and the world went grey, then black.

Anna dreamt about stroking the creature's fur and listening to its strange purring as she fell asleep. She woke up cold and alone, and started to get up, intending to go back up to her bedsit, but instead found herself in a small cell with bars in the window. And that's when the pain hit her.

As Anna screamed in vain to God and the Devil to take the pain away, the thing in the underbelly of her building scuttled back through its gateway into the hell from which it had come, and settled down to sleep. By the time it would wake up, Anna's suffering would long be over.

TEA WITH THE DEVIL

The street was strangely quiet for Halloween. No trick-or-treaters as far as the eye could see, and even the candles in the carved pumpkins had been extinguished by a wind that appeared from nowhere and disappeared again just as fast. It was early evening and the light had all but faded from the dirty urban sky. There was a distinct chill in the autumn air and for a moment the street seemed quite deserted. Then a flurry of footsteps and a tall man wearing a long coat, with a cap pulled down tightly over his ears, rounded the corner at great speed. Close on his heels came three youths, hatred in their eyes and baseball bats in their hands.

The man disappeared round the side of a large block of flats and the youths followed, pausing when they realised that he had entered the building.

Once inside the block of flats, the tall man headed straight for a flat on the ground floor and pounded on the door. An eye appeared in the peephole and the door opened, the man inside delighted to see his old friend.

"What a wonderful surprise, come on in!" An energetic, grey-haired man in his early sixties was holding open the door, smiling at his unexpected guest. "How long's it been now?"

The tall man quickly pushed his host inside, leapt across the threshold and slammed the door behind him.

"I'm being chased," panted the new arrival. His host looked surprised.

"Oh," he said, pointing to his guest's head, "did they notice your ... um...?"

The tall man pulled off his cap, revealing a fine, if rather tussled, head of shoulder length black hair. As he smoothed it down, through his hair poked two perfect little horns.

"No. Definitely not," the tall man shook his head. "I had my cap on all the time." He took off his coat. His host took it from him and hung it on a coat rack, then turned to his guest and pointed at his backside.

"Perhaps it popped out from under your coat?" he suggested helpfully. The tall man glanced down, over his shoulder. He was wearing an elegant, if somewhat worn set of black tails. From the slit at the back protruded a long, thick tail with a fluffy black tip. The tall man smoothed down his tail.

"It couldn't have," he said. "My coat is very long. They couldn't have seen it. In any case, there are a lot of strange looking fellows out tonight."

"Then what on earth happened?" asked his host, a look of concern on his amiable face.

"I really have no idea. Some louts threw themselves at me. Each one shouted something different. One of them yelled 'Fucking Gyppo!' Another one, 'Yids to the gas!' And the third,

'Fuck off back to where you come from, you fucking nigger wop!' Do you understand any of this?"

"Well, the 'nigger wop' you must have misheard. But, all in all, I guess you don't look quite like the rest of us. You're complexion is kind of dusky, and not everyone likes that around here."

"Oh well, in that case there's nothing more to be said." The tall man relaxed a little and smiled at his host. "And what about you? Has your collection grown since I last saw you?"

"Oh yes, it's definitely grown!" The grey-haired man positively beamed. "Would you like to see?"

"Of course. You know that I enjoy looking at depictions of my fellows."

The grey-haired man took his friend around the large flat, proudly displaying new additions to his exceptionally fine collection of devils: painted devils, wooden devils, bronze devils, cuddly devils, scary devils, big devils and small devils.

The tall man smiled as he contemplated all these likenesses of himself and other fiends. It seemed to him that since God had created mankind, people had been fascinated with the fallen angels, just as the fallen angels were drawn to people. The difference was, of course, that the fallen angels were jealous of people – of their closeness to God, whereas people had nothing to be jealous of.

Finally the grey-haired man led his guest to his prized new acquisition – a small oil painting hanging at the far end of the sitting room. It portrayed a group of men on horseback, silhouetted against a twilit sky. They rode slowly through a forest, their horses tired and their heads hung low. Some had rifles strapped to their saddles. Just visible on the head of the last rider were two small horns.

"Oh, I don't believe I recognise this fellow," said the tall man, studying the painting closely. "He's not one of our original lot."

"No, indeed. This one started off human."

"Ah, that would explain it," the tall man mused, "but what's he doing riding with men?"

"They're Polish partisans," explained his host, "fighting the Nazis."

"Ah yes, the Nazis... But why does a devil ride with partisans? That kind of co-mingling isn't strictly allowed, you know. We're supposed to remain neutral."

"It's a very interesting story." The grey-haired man was excited about having got his friend's attention. "It was told to me in an antique shop by the old Pole who sold me the painting. It will be my pleasure to relate it to you, should you wish to hear it."

"Please do." His host's enthusiasm for all things devilish touched Lucifer deeply. The grey-haired man looked delighted.

"Well, it all began in a small Polish village in the seventeenth century. In the village lived a peasant called Boruta. He was a God-fearing man ... oops!" He threw his guest an apologetic glance. The devil smiled back benevolently and shrugged his shoulders. His friend carried on with his tale.

"He was a hardworking man, well-liked by the other peasants and respected for his incredible strength. One day, when King Jan the Third was travelling through the countryside to visit his mistress, his carriage got stuck in mud near a field in which Boruta was working. The king's servants pushed and pulled, and beat the horses, but the carriage did not shift. Boruta spotted their plight and hurried over. The peasant braced his shoulders and single-handedly pushed the king's carriage out of the mud. So impressed was the king with Boruta's strength that he rewarded him with land and a title. But, like many people who move rapidly from poverty to riches, Boruta did not take well to his newly acquired wealth. He was a cruel and dissolute lord; he beat his peasants and indulged in every conceivable vice. He stopped going to church and insulted the parish priest when he tried to visit his manor. So vile did Boruta become that when he died, he was sent back into the world as a devil, destined forever to haunt the marshes and forests around his village, frightening maids and luring men into the chest high bogs."

The devil smiled, evidently enjoying his friend's tale. The grey-haired man continued.

"A couple of hundred years went by and Boruta got bored out in the marshes. Scaring the villagers wasn't enough for him anymore. Then one Sunday in May he heard the church bells ringing and crept to the edge of the forest to watch the people going to their temple. How pathetic they all looked – dressed up to the nines, sucking up to the equally pathetic parish priest (a different one now, of course, to the one that Boruta had thrown out of his manor all those years ago). What empty ritual. Boruta wondered how they would look if the church tower they were all so proud of were to fall down. That gave him the idea he needed. Now he had a mission.

"Boruta waited until dark and then set about his plan to bring down the church tower. He climbed on it and shook it, but the structure would not budge. He howled and scratched, but nothing happened. He struck at the tower all night with his powerful tail and finally succeeded in knocking off a couple of roof tiles. The following morning the priest prayed, the women wailed and the men fixed the roof tiles. That night Boruta went back to the church and pawed at the tower with his strong curved claws. He managed to inflict some visible scratches, but that was all. The next day the priest prayed and the people prayed, and Boruta waited until nightfall to resume his attack on the tower.

"For a hundred years the devil attacked the tower, and the villagers prayed to God for salvation from the unholy creature that kept them awake at night with his howling and scratching. For a hundred years the tower stood proud on the little church and did not succumb to the devil's attacks. But then war came to Poland. Not for the first time, of course, because Poland had seen many wars and had even on occasion ceased to exist as a country in its own right, but Boruta's small village had remained pretty much intact; too insignificant to warrant the attention of invading forces. But this time things were different.

"The Nazis swept through the country in search of Jews and Gypsies, scholars and priests, and anyone else they didn't like. And so it came to pass that they arrived in the small village. They couldn't find any Jews or scholars or Gypsies, but they pulled the priest out of his church and shot him in front of the villagers, and then they proceeded to blow up the ancient church tower. Smoke and rubble flew in all directions, and orange flames leapt up to heaven.

"Boruta gazed at the church in disbelief. It looked strange – wrong. The mighty tower, disproportionately large for the small church it had adorned, lay shattered into a thousand pieces all over the ground. The tower that Boruta had scratched and shaken and pummelled with his tail for a hundred years was no more. The devil looked at the rubble and wept. He sat on the ground, curled his fine tail under his body, and wept and wept. Then he disappeared. But rumours spread through the surrounding area of a brave partisan riding against the Nazis at night – a partisan with a pair of horns and a long black tail."

The grey-haired man smiled at his friend.

"A fine tale," responded the devil, "and a fine painting. I'm pleased it has found its way into your wonderful museum".

"Thank you, my friend," said the grey-haired man and, the tour being over, the two of them retired to a small parlour, the host beaming even more than earlier.

"You've no idea how happy it makes me that you like my collection. But surely you're not in a hurry? Surely you can stay for tea? I have some lovely biscuits."

"You're such a strange species," the devil mused. "Kind, generous, civilised, so many great achievements, and yet so brutal, cruel and blood thirsty – for no real reason. There are enough resources on earth to go around for everyone, and enough capable people to run things, and yet the world is in a terrible state."

The host studied his old friend carefully.

"You don't seem quite yourself today. You should be celebrating."

"And why is that?" the devil asked.

"Precisely because there are terrible things going on in the world today. People are killing each other for nothing. There's so much evil in the world. You should be proud!"

183

"Proud of what? I didn't invent the atom bomb. I didn't come up with the Holocaust, or with ethnic cleansing, the Tutsi massacre or any of those things…"

"And what happened recently in the Balkans, and Iraq," added the grey-haired man, "and all the bombings, and what's going on in Syria right now… The world's a right devils' playground."

"Mr John," the tall man glanced at this friend with a hint of disapproval in his dark eyes, "please don't insult us. We don't torture children – they haven't had time to sin yet. We don't rape little girls or build death camps."

The grey-haired man studied his friend thoughtfully for a moment.

"I'll bring us some tea," he said, and left the devil to his thoughts.

The devil walked over to the window, pulled back the net curtain a fraction and peered outside. He noticed his tormentors hanging around, smoking cigarettes and watching the building. He quickly let the curtain drop and moved away from the window. John entered, bringing a tea tray, which he set down before them, pouring a cup and passing it to his guest along with a chocolate chip cookie.

"You don't look too good, Mr Lucifer," he eyed his friend sympathetically. "You mustn't worry, everything will be fine. That is, what I meant to say was, everything will be bad and then even worse."

"You're a nice man, Mr John. To be honest, I have a great favour to ask you."

"Oh no, not that. I'm very fond of you – you know I am. But I won't give you my soul. No way!"

"No, no. It's not about your soul. We have too many souls at the moment. Can't get rid of them. Once upon a time you had to resort to temptation – great wealth, limitless knowledge, beautiful women … those were the days… Now they'll give their soul away for a lousy buck, or for free. There are no more Fausts, Mr John – those times are long gone."

"Well, what is it then?"

Lucifer frowned as a door slammed outside the flat.

"How should I put it?" he continued. "It's about justice. People are doing terrible things, soon they'll demolish the whole earth, the end of the world will come and they will be saved. We rebelled once, a long time ago, soon we will be out of work, and we would like – how should I put it? – to be saved as well."

"But Mr Lucifer, that's quite impossible!" Both men looked round nervously as the sound of raised voices reverberated on the landing outside the flat. "In any case, how exactly do you think I can help you?"

"I heard that a Polish philosopher once wrote something on the subject – well, that, er, that the devil can be saved. And I would be most grateful if you could find out how this could be done. Perhaps I could drop by again – in a few days' time?"

The voices outside were louder now, much closer. Lucifer listened uneasily. Just then, there came a loud pounding on the door.

"It's them!" cried Lucifer. "Damn! They could kill you. Listen carefully: I will lure them away from here, and you hide. Or get some help!"

Before John had a chance to respond, Lucifer pulled on his hat and coat with lightning speed, opened the door and bolted out, straight into the arms of the waiting thugs. The youths were caught off guard and Lucifer slipped through, running as fast as he could away from John's building.

The youths chased Lucifer through the dark streets. If trick-or-treaters had tried their luck in this part of town, they were certainly gone now – probably tucked up in bed, stomachs full of sweets. Rounding a corner, Lucifer stopped suddenly, letting past a malnourished young woman carrying a small child and pulling another, slightly larger, child along behind her.

The youths did not slow down. They knocked over the woman and children, and leapt on Lucifer, beating him mercilessly with their baseball bats.

The woman pulled herself off the ground, picked up the child that had fallen from her arms, and started to run away. The other child ran after her, crying loudly.

Lucifer's mangled body had stopped moving. One of the youths held a horn torn from Lucifer's skull to his own forehead, his victim's blood dripping from it and smearing the killer's leering face. Another youth laughed loudly as his companion cut off Lucifer's tail and made several clumsy attempts to use it as a skipping rope.

The boys heard an approaching police siren and, grabbing their trophies, disappeared giggling around the corner.

"A bit old to be trick-or-treating, wasn't he?" Officer Fullerton commented to his colleague as he finished his unsuccessful search for a pulse and straightened up, staring uncomprehendingly at the mutilated remains.

Lucifer's unseeing eyes were fixed on the dark heavens and the distant stars as his earthly life bled out into the dust of the gutter.

ELEGY

Black smoke curls up from the oil lamp, its meagre contents nearly spent. The writer sits at the makeshift desk. Darkness crouches over him. The hunger pangs subside as he dips the nib in the ink well and his mind begins to soar. Faces form out of the mist, and smile. Benevolent eyes observe him from a past as distant as the stars above the jagged walls.

His father bred birds in the barn; their feathers would float down softly and the whir of their wings soothed the boy as he lay on the scented hay below. Sunny days pour onto the page. Endless days of summer. Rachel with hair like the ravens that roosted in the ancient linden tree by the graveyard. Rachel with a face like the winter moon, hurrying home from the synagogue. The scent of fresh bread mingling with meadow flowers in the sultry air. His mother baked bread in the bakery, his father was an artist – the village eccentric, as people were wont to say.

A drop of ink as blue-black as the night falls from the writer's pen as a train rattles past. From its tiny, barb-wired windows skeleton hands reach towards a pitiless moon. Memories creep into the tiny room. Visions of a half-forgotten childhood – as alien as a foreign land – steal in through the cracks. They stir about the writer; half-formed figures of neighbours and loved ones, of village elders and childhood friends. He knows that he will follow them soon – into a place with no windows. Only his grandfather cheated the emissaries of Hate and Fire, with their heavy boots and voices like thunder. Grandfather, who defied their poison showers and furnaces, and picked his own time to depart – sitting down in his favourite chair and telling his heart to stop. Grandfather, who lived to ninety-two, and could have lived to a hundred and fifty thanks to the water from Old Simon's lake.

When the writer was twelve years old, his grandfather fell gravely ill. The Doctor prophesied another two days of life – perhaps three – and bid the family say their goodbyes. The boy's mother tried to make him understand that Grandfather would be leaving them, and that the boy should spend these last moments by the old man's bed. The boy burst into tears, wailing something about a magic lake, then ran from the house.

"It's just a story!" His father called after him, but the boy was gone.

A hundred years ago, Old Simon owned a tavern on a forest road – a cheerful place where a weary traveller could water his horse, rest his feet, and eat a simple, honest meal. After dinner, Old Simon would play the fiddle and his daughter Esterka would sing. Esterka had the voice of an angel and a delicate, pale face, ringed by velvet tresses as black as night. She was like a fragile flower, which the sun and wind took care not to visit too roughly. Even the coldest heart melted when that gentle, unearthly young girl sang. Tales of her beauty and her divine voice spread quickly through the countryside, and it was rumoured that the king himself rode in disguise to hear her sing.

Then one day the world turned to hate and fire. Enemies attacked from without; turmoil erupted within. Brother turned against brother, neighbour against neighbour, Gentile against Jew. It wasn't long before a pogrom tore through the region. Soldiers and peasants marched with burning torches against those who dressed differently, or prayed differently, or sang a different song.

Old Simon saw the baying mob coming across the fields; the hate burning in their eyes, the fire burning in their clenched fists. A great fear for his beloved Esterka seized his heart. The shouting men drew closer, their anger and lust fuelled by local ale. Old Simon put his arms around his only child, and prayed to the Lord to save her and to spare their home from the hate and the fire.

As the frenzied horde gathered before the inn, a terrible creaking sound arose and echoed around the forest. The ground shuddered, the tavern walls started to tremble, the earth opened up and water gushed forth around the old building. Then, before the hate-filled eyes of the crowd, Old Simon's tavern sank in its entirety into the earth and water, taking Simon and Esterka with it, and leaving behind a dark, restless lake.

The rabble looked on in fear. Some turned and fled; others fell to their knees and made the sign of the cross. But no more Jewish homes were burned that night, or for many nights to come. It was as though those brooding waters had extinguished the hate and the fire that had kindled in fallible, hollow hearts.

For years to come, the peasants avoided the lake and the path that led to it, finding other ways to traverse the forest. Soon the dirt track all but vanished, as trees and bushes reclaimed the land, and reeds grew around the dark body of water. But rumours sprang up: of a magical lake hidden deep in the forest – a drop of water from it could heal a wound, and a mouthful could cure an ailing man from the most perfidious disease.

So it was that the boy set off to bring back some of the life-saving water for his grandfather. He knew the woods around his parents' village, but beyond his usual haunts the forest was dark, even in daylight. The vegetation grew thick and high, and strange rustling noises all around him made the tiny hairs on the back of the boy's neck stand on end – like fur on a startled cat. More than once he got the feeling that he was being followed, but he could see no one. With no familiar landmarks to guide him, he plunged ever deeper into the unknown. After a long and tiring march, it dawned on him that he was completely lost. It was a dry summer, and there was no sign of a lake or any other water. Fear and despair overcame the boy. He sat down on the fallen trunk of an ancient oak, looked down at the wooden bowl he'd taken from his mother's kitchen, and began to cry.

In between sobs, the boy became aware of a strange sound drifting through the forest. It was high pitched and distant, and at first he thought it was the wind blowing through the branches of the trees above him, but then he realised that it was a human voice – a girl's voice, singing. He stood up, wiping his eyes with the back of his hand, and called out.

"Hello?" Silence. "Is there anybody there?" Nothing. And then the singing came again, stronger this time, haunting and beautiful. The boy tried to determine its source. It seemed to be coming from somewhere directly ahead, and he walked towards it – slowly. The boy's mother had sung to him when he was little – her voice was soft and sweet. But the voice that came to him now from the depths of the forest was like nothing he'd ever heard before. It was as if an angel were guiding him through the verdant darkness, drowning out the frightening sounds of forest creatures scampering around the lost child.

It wasn't long before the boy saw a dim light ahead. There was a clearing in the forest, and the sunlight had managed to filter through. The boy could see reeds in front of him: cattails and long, feathery grasses shimmering in the mottled light. As he reached them, and pushed a few aside so that he could see past, the singing stopped. Peering intently through the reeds, he beheld an incredible sight. Before him spread a body of murky water. Here and there the sunlight cast diamonds on its surface, but mostly the lake had an inky hue. Despite the stillness of the air, the waters of the lake were fitful with constant motion.

The boy became aware of the urgent rustling of the reeds all around him. Creeping forward, he bent down cautiously to scoop up some of the precious liquid. As he did so, a shaft of sunlight caught on the water pouring into the bowl, and it sparkled like a handful of diamonds. The awestricken boy realised that he'd been holding his breath, and exhaled deeply. He took one last look at the magical, dark, luminescent, foreboding, uplifting place; then turned away. He held the bowl in one hand, covering its priceless contents with the other. Careful not to trip and spill his prize, he headed for home. Somehow this time his feet knew which way to go.

"Where have you been!?" The boy's mother greeted him with tears in her eyes; angry, happy and relieved in equal measure.

"I have to see Grandpa," the boy stated firmly, the determination in his voice stifling his mother's imminent outburst, and causing both parents to stand aside and let him pass.

When the boy confided in his father a few days later and led him to the clearing in the forest, there was no sign of a lake to be seen. Only a couple of dried out reeds whispering something that human ears could not hear.

A shot outside, a scream, the walls shift like a street of crocodiles. The writer trembles as his mother's cool hand touches his gaunt cheek, her smile like a forbidden song. The oil-lamp flickers, the night darkens, vultures gather around the broken souls that mill around the midnight room. The writer struggles to keep his mother's face in mind, but the darkness swallows it, as the echo of running footsteps reverberates outside.

Elegy

The writer pauses, listening; ink drops fall from his pen like tears. They are liquidating the ghetto. Soon he will be led away along cobblestones that will leap out of the ground in pity. *Even the stones were moved by their plight* – an old Gentile peasant will tell a documentary film crew sixty years later – *but not the rock-hearted men who led them away*... Soon a lively foxtrot blasted from tinny speakers will silence the gunshots as Death and the Devil observe their handiwork over the shoulders of a dozen boy-faced butchers... Soon his forefathers will cradle him in their bony arms and pass him lovingly from embrace to embrace; their eyes full of sorrow. They weep for him and bemoan the rapacious beast-fate that lies in wait: the destiny that looms because he is of their flesh and blood. The journey into the night and fog for he is born of them. Soon the writer will ascend to an indifferent heaven, like the black smoke from his oil lamp.

BAGPUSS

The train journey was exhausting. The removal company was going to deliver most of their things, but even the basics that Emily's mother had insisted they take themselves filled three heavy suitcases, a hold-all and several ungainly plastic bags. Miraculously they had managed to load everything onto the train before it departed, but Emily couldn't stop worrying about how they would get it all off at the other end. She dozed off during the long ride, but her sleep was fitful, her anxiety giving rise to a horrible dream. Not only were they unable to get all the luggage off on time, but her mother disappeared and the train left with Emily and her pet still on it, taking them to a dark, deserted

193

place, where she got separated from Bagpuss and didn't know how to get home. From this she awoke sweating and headachy.

"What is it, dear?" asked her mother, in that tired, indifferent tone that had been in her voice ever since Emily's father had walked out one day and never come back.

"Nothing," said Emily, relieved that it had been just a dream. Her worries still played on her mind though. She moved the cat carrier slightly and peered in through the bars at Bagpuss, who meowed – a plaintive, pathetic, frightened little noise, cute in a kitten perhaps, but strangely unnerving in a large, lazy, eight-year-old tabby lap-cat. Bagpuss had been emitting similar sounds ever since Emily and her mother had forced him into the blue cat carrier. He had struggled with all his might, wedging his paws against the plastic around the opening of the box and tensing up his entire body with strength extraordinary for a being a fraction of the size of the two humans trying to push him in. But as soon as the battle was lost and the bars of the cat carrier came down before his eyes, he started mewling in the tiny yet penetrating way of an unwanted kitten destined for a stone-laden sack at the bottom of a lake.

"It's okay," Emily told him, "I'm here. I won't let anything bad happen to you."

Bagpuss had been with Emily since he was six weeks old, but he had been silent as a kitten, and had only found his tongue at a later age, sparsely using a low, gruff meow to indicate that he was hungry or wanted to go outdoors. Mostly, he would lie on Emily's lap, purring loudly and sometimes even snoring. So the eerie little squeaks and cries were something new and distressing to his twelve-year-old mistress – as new and distressing as having to leave her city life and move to the countryside, away from her room, her house, her street, and everything that made her feel safe. New things, new places, new people had no appeal to her; they gave her a nasty tight sensation in the pit of her stomach – a feeling like something really bad was about to happen; a feeling that had increased in frequency since her father had left. Now that they were on the train and heading for her new home, the feeling of impending doom was stronger than ever, and Emily was convinced that Bagpuss felt it too.

"How many more stations before we get there?" Emily asked her mother.

"I don't know, dear."

"You have to ask someone, mummy."

"Why?"

"We have to get ready to get off the train before it reaches the station. Otherwise we won't have time to get everything off."

"Of course we will."

"But we have to get ready before we get to the station, mummy."

Emily's agitation was starting to break through the protective barrier of Valium, and worry her mother. The child had always been timid and oversensitive, but lately she was stressing about everything. Emily's mother tried to remember being twelve. She had been brought up in the countryside and remembered her childhood as being full of sunny days – helping on the farm, cycling with her friends, running down to the river to fish or remove socks and shoes and paddle – unstressed and carefree. Not like Emily, who always fretted about everything. And her father leaving had provided the perfect opportunity for the child's anxiety to run wild. Perhaps life in the country would be good for the girl. Perhaps a new start in life was what they both needed.

As they pulled into the village station, all their things were already by the train door – at Emily's insistence, of course – and Emily was firmly clutching Bagpuss's cat carrier to her chest.

"Mummy, I'll go first and put Bagpuss down, and then I'll help you get the suitcases down, but you'll have to pass them to me because I don't want to leave Bagpuss on his own on the platform because someone might steal him."

"Nobody's going to steal Bagpuss."

"Well, a dog might attack the cat carrier and Bagpuss might get hurt."

"Nothing's going to happen to Bagpuss," sighed Emily's mother.

"Yes, but you don't know that, mummy. I have to stay on the platform with him to make sure he doesn't think we've abandoned him and get scared."

"Very well, Emily. You stay on the platform with Bagpuss and I'll pass the bags down to you."

The unloading went smoothly, apart from Bagpuss's desperate mewling as his miniature prison got moved again and the cat temporarily lost the ground under his feet, his whole world shaking and lurching until Emily placed the carrier down on the platform – on solid ground now, but still imprisoned and claustrophobic.

There were no cabs at the station, but the station master phoned for one and, after a long wait, a man in his sixties arrived and somehow helped them load all their belongings into his battered old Ford. The man chatted away to Emily's mother and eyed her with an interest that made Emily nervous. The girl ignored the cab driver, and concentrated her attentions on Bagpuss, who had fallen deathly quiet in his sweaty prison.

"It's a ten-minute drive," her mother had told her, and five minutes into the journey the feeling of impending doom in Emily's stomach had grown to a level which made her want to clutch her abdomen. Instead, she hugged Bagpuss's cage tightly. The cat yelped, and Emily was certain that he was sharing her fear of what was to come.

Five minutes later, and the three of them – Emily, Emily's mother and Bagpuss in his plastic cage – were standing in front of their new home. Emily's mother had turned down the cab driver's repeated offer of helping them carry their bags into the house, but had taken the business card on the back of which he had jotted his home phone number. And Emily finally understood the feeling in the pit of her stomach that she'd had since she was little – the feeling that crept over her in the middle of the day or in the dead of night; the feeling that grew as she tossed and turned in her bed – formless and indescribable until it took shape and found expression in her nightmares and anxiety dreams: those dreams of finding ourselves naked in front of others, of facing an examination paper without knowing the curriculum, of fleeing something unspeakable along corridors that get narrower and narrower until we can scarcely breathe...

Emily trembled as she looked up at her new home, and knew that the recurrent feelings of impending doom had all led to this: the brooding dark house whose eaves cast a shadow that somehow managed to reach her and make her shiver on this fine summer afternoon. A house whose gloomy corners would devour her, and her mother and her cat. Even the roses climbing ramshackle up the walls of the house were the colour of congealed blood, their scent suffocating, their thorns waiting to scar anyone who came close. But worse still – worse than the house with its bloody roses and windows gaping like cataract-covered eyes – was the untamed expanse of land behind the building. A wilderness of plants, spiky and barbed, ready to impale anyone who ventured among them. Tangled roots ready to wind themselves around an ankle and bring its owner crashing into the spider-infested undergrowth. A place teeming with unseen life, a thousand creatures – scurrying, crawling, watching, waiting. And beyond all that: a dark tree line looming ominously on the horizon.

Emily felt faint. All she had ever known were the familiar streets of the city in which she had lived all her life – streets with names that made sense and instilled a feeling of security: First Avenue, Second Avenue, Third Avenue; streets that criss-crossed each other at reliable right-angles, forming orderly squares with houses and shops where they intersected. Even the parks were safe – the grass neatly mown, the trees arranged symmetrically, planted evenly apart, their branches trimmed regularly so that they could not grow into monstrous limbs that reached for you and tried to drag you into a scratching, deadly embrace... Velvety moss, scented wild herbs and colourful meadow flowers brought Emily no comfort. What should have been a Garden of Eden was to Emily a Garden of Evil.

Bagpuss mewed wildly in his cat carrier – no longer a tiny, pitiful squeal, but a feral, desperate cry – and threw himself against the bars, rattling the plastic cage so hard that Emily feared it would overturn and harm her pet. She carried the box with the wailing, thrashing animal up to the house and, once her mother unlocked the door, inside. Emily made sure the front door was securely closed again, put down the cage and opened it carefully. Bagpuss sprang out faster than Emily thought possible, and headed straight for the front door, scratching at it feverishly.

"You'd better let him out," Emily's mother told her. "I have to open the door in any case, to bring our bags in."

"But mummy…"

"He'll be fine."

"Okay. But I'll go with him."

"Don't you want to have a look around the house?"

Emily cast a fearful glance past her mother, at the murky hallway with doors leading off it, and the winding staircase leading up into darkness.

"Maybe later," she told her mother and turned her attention back to her frantically meowing, scratching cat.

As soon as Emily opened the front door, Bagpuss bolted out like the proverbial bat out of hell and took off down the porch steps.

"Bagpuss, wait!"

The cat reached the bottom of the steps and paused, looking around, sniffing the air, droopy whiskers and fluffy tail twitching nervously. Bagpuss had never known a world such as this. His cruel imprisonment in the evil-smelling plastic cage was all but forgotten, as a universe of magnificent scents, sights and sounds burst open all around him. It was as though he had sleepwalked through his life and now, finally, he was wide awake – his nerves tingling with excitement and the blood singing in his veins.

Bagpuss hardly noticed as Emily caught up with him and spoke to him softly.

"There you are, Bagpuss." Emily reached down and stroked the cat gently. Bagpuss became aware of his friend next to him, and looked up at her, purring loudly. He could smell the lush scent of the roses clinging to the walls of the house behind him. He could smell wild flowers and herbs, birds, mice and other small creatures in the bushes all around. But Bagpuss could smell something else too – an alluring, intoxicating scent, and it was calling him. The cat quivered from the tip of his pink nose to the tip of his black and grey tail, then set off at a trot.

"Bagpuss, wait!" Emily ran after her pet, terrified of losing sight of him. She found him standing behind the house, gazing across the expanse of meadow towards the woods on the horizon. Bagpuss's nose twitched as he took in that wonderful scent – it was the fragrance of the warm grass before him, it was the scent of open space – the smell of freedom. He took off across the field.

"No, Bagpuss! You're going too far!" Emily followed her cat, trying not to fall as the branches of strange plants curled around her ankles; increasingly distressed as she kept losing sight of the cat in the tall grass.

As Bagpuss bounded over the exotic landscape, the breeze ruffled his fur, and the sounds of birdsong and of small frightened creatures scurrying away through the grass caressed his ears. Even through all the new aromas of plants and animals, Bagpuss noticed another, stronger smell. He slowed down, years of dozing on Emily's sofa having taken their toll on his natural feline stamina, but continued to press ahead, until the strange new scent was joined by a rushing, gurgling sound. As he navigated the last few metres of grass between him and the noisy thing ahead, Emily cried out behind him.

"Oh my God! No, Bagpuss, no!"

But Bagpuss had already burst out onto the riverbank, and was staring down at the river – narrow at this point, only a few metres across – silver and blue-grey, light dancing between the brown and dark green reflections of the trees that grew on its other side.

As the cat stared in awe at the flowing water, the dancing light, he caught sight of movement made by something more solid – it was a fish. Bagpuss carefully made his way down to the water and contemplated sticking in a paw.

"Bagpuss, no!" In the second that it took Bagpuss to glance back at Emily, the fish was gone. Then Emily was picking him up, enveloping him gently in her arms, her scent familiar and soporific.

"You mustn't go near the river, it's not safe." Bagpuss was disappointed to be leaving the riverbank, but he was tired now, and after an initial half-hearted squirm, he allowed himself to be carried back to the house.

That night it took Emily a long time to get to sleep. The latter part of the day had passed uneventfully, apart from unpacking their suitcases and bags. The men from the removal company were not due until the following morning, and Emily's mother had brought enough food to do the three of them for dinner and for breakfast the following day. Emily had nervously explored the house, and put away the few items of clothing that she had brought with her in the large old wardrobe of the room that her mother had chosen for her. The room was sombre enough during the day, but at night darkness lay thick in its nooks and crannies, and the tree outside sent restless shadows scuttling over Emily's window and scratched at the glass panes when the breeze stirred it. When the last light had faded from the sky, the darkness outside was profound – nothing like the polluted orange glow of city night. Emily pulled her blanket up to her chin and listened fearfully to the silence, broken only by Bagpuss snoring at the foot of her bed – but even the comforting sound of the sleeping cat did little to still Emily's racing heart.

When she finally fell asleep, Emily dreamt of the frightening expanse of land leading down to the river behind the house and the verdant darkness of the woods beyond. She was trying to keep sight of Bagpuss among the long grass and meadow flowers. It was magic hour, and the field around Emily glowed in the eerie, beautiful, alien light. The smell of the flowers and wild herbs was at its strongest, the sultry remains of the hot day enhancing the various scents, making them intoxicating, stifling.

"Bagpuss! Wait!" As Emily hurried in the direction where she had just seen the tip of Bagpuss's tail disappear, she became aware that she was not alone out here with her cat. She slowed down, looking around nervously, and shrieked as a flash of dry lightning lit up the field and she spotted eyes in the grass, all around, watching her. Emily started to panic, glancing this way and that, and the hundreds of cornflowers stared back at her, their piercing cornflower eyes unnaturally blue in the strange light, staring at Emily suspiciously, accusingly, as if they knew something about her that she didn't know herself.

Emily trembled, then, seeing her cat leaping over a clump of dandelions some way ahead, she moved to head off after him, but stopped again as an ear-rending screech silenced the insects in the grass nearby. Emily looked around fearfully. The screech came again, and that was when she saw the poppy. The flower stared at Emily, then swayed from side to side on its stem until it seemed to haemorrhage into a cockerel with deep red plumage and a scarlet crest. As Emily watched, horrified, the thing continued to shake itself violently until its crest dripped blood, rending open its fear-poisoned beak and screaming at Emily until she turned and raced towards the river and the dark tree line beyond. As she ran, Emily noticed the single ears of wild barley growing here and there in the field. She tried to skirt around one, but skimmed it with her foot and stopped as the plant glistened with a golden hue. Emily stared as the plant bristled its husks angrily and, emitting a hollow rattling sound, ground itself into a golden hedgehog and ran from her, pricking the slender wild herbs that stood in its way.

Emily clapped her hands to her temples and headed for the river, a terrible fear for Bagpuss rising within her. As soon as it had come, magic hour was over, and the last of the light bled from the sky. As Emily reached the bank of the river she heard a loud splash and she cried out.

"Bagpuss! Bagpuss!" But there was no answer, no familiar meow, only a faint splash in the river some distance away. Emily stared into the inky depths of the river and finally she saw Bagpuss – a little way off, his paws flailing helplessly as he tried to stay afloat. As Emily jumped into the cold river, an undercurrent suddenly caught Bagpuss and pulled him under the dark water. Emily screamed and threw herself in the direction of her beloved pet. For a moment Bagpuss's head bobbed up above the water and Emily half-swam half-ran towards him, but the current got a hold of him and carried him away downstream. Tears streaming down her face, Emily swam after her cat.

Darkness had set in fast and Emily could hardly distinguish the black water from the blackness all around her. She could just make out Bagpuss ahead of her, tossed about by the current. With a huge effort she finally reached him and pulled him out of the water, clutching him to her, and managed to get him to the shore. Wet through, he was no longer big and fluffy, but small and vulnerable. She tried to warm his little body against her neck and shoulder, but he was stone cold and limp.

"Wake up, Bagpuss, wake up!" she begged, but it was too late. Emily cried and cried, and hugged Bagpuss's dead body until she woke up to find her pet very much alive, his nose pressed up against her face, eyeing her with a look of concern.

"Oh, Bagpuss," cried Emily and squeezed the surprised cat until he yelped and removed himself to the armchair in the corner of the room.

The next morning Bagpuss woke Emily bright and early, demanding to be let out. Emily refused to open the front door and clapped her hands over her ears, ignoring the cat's urgent meowing. It wasn't until Emily's mother found a pool of cat pee by the front door that Emily was reprimanded and, after much debate and tear shedding, Bagpuss was allowed to explore the boundlessness of the land behind the house once more.

The men from the removal company arrived with the rest of the clothes, the furniture, kitchen utensils, Emily's prized collection of stones and pebbles – which Emily laid out according to size on the large windowsill in her bedroom – and the thing that Emily had been waiting for most: Bagpuss's cat litter. Emily hoped that Bagpuss would start relieving himself in the litter again, and wouldn't need to leave the house. But her hopes were dashed, as the cat spurned the litter entirely and spent all of the time that he was awake either outdoors or sitting by the front door, begging to be let out.

As time wore on, Emily found herself increasingly alone. Bagpuss no longer sat on her lap or played with the cloth mouse that she sometimes dragged around in front of him on a piece of string. He still slept in Emily's room, but he was coming home increasingly late and demanding to be let out increasingly early. During the day, Emily would try to follow Bagpuss, spending as much time outdoors – among the heady-scented flowers and crawling insects – as her mother would allow, trying to make sure that nothing happened to her cat. But when Emily's mother insisted on her doing chores or accompanying her to the village grocery store or doing some homework in preparation for the beginning of term in her new school once summer was over, Emily spent every moment worrying about Bagpuss. When her mother made her go to bed before Bagpuss had come home, Emily would lie awake, her mind conjuring up blood-curdling images of her beloved pet drowning, being torn apart by foxes, being decapitated by local juvenile delinquents fancying themselves as Satanists, being bitten by a rabid bat or getting stuck in a rabbit hole and starving to death. In those dark, lonely hours Emily imagined every horror possible – except...

The car was a brand new bottle-green Land Rover driven by a twenty-four-year-old banker. It was difficult to put the SUV through its paces in London – too many speed cameras – but the winding country lanes in this part of the world were just bliss. You could easily do the curves at 90 miles an hour, and the straight stretches of road ... well ... there was no limit – only the size of your balls.

The mouse was small and grey, and running for its life. Bagpuss could tell that it was tiring and he fancied his chances. All the time he had spent roaming the wilderness behind the house and chasing any critter that was smaller than him had paid off. A firm layer of muscle had replaced his portliness, and his senses were no longer dulled by hours of snoozing in front of the telly. So far he had caught nothing, but today all that was going to change. He'd nail the damned mouse, but he wouldn't eat it himself; he would carry it up to Emily's room and place it on her bed to show her how much he loved her.

The mouse sprinted past the house, Bagpuss hot on its tail. Blind with fear, the mouse burst out onto the main road that led to the village, and the cat leapt after it. The impact with the metal grille threw Bagpuss into the air and he landed in the road, the Land Rover's shining silver alloy wheels directing the entire weight of the vehicle onto his small furry body. The SUV didn't even slow down. The mouse disappeared into the undergrowth on the far side of the road and, as dusk fell, a fox snatched up what was left of Bagpuss and carried it back to its hungry family.

Emily waited for Bagpuss to come home. She polished her stones and pebbles over and over, hardly aware of what she was doing. At midnight her mother caught her trying to sneak out of the house to look for her pet and sent her, wailing, up to bed. Emily spent most of the night peering out of her window into the darkness beyond, and eventually cried herself to sleep as the dawn chorus started up outside her window.

The days that followed were akin to a never-ending version of one of Emily's anxiety dreams. She spent every free moment of daytime wandering around the wasteland at the back of the house, calling Bagpuss's name. At night, the silence was unbearable, the tree outside her window scratched the glass like nails on a chalkboard and the shadows in her room crowded around her menacingly. Ever since her father had left, Bagpuss had slept in Emily's room, his snoring making her giggle, but never keeping her awake for long. And as with the time after her father had first departed, Emily was in a permanent state of suspension – waiting rather than living – the anxious feeling in her stomach making her nauseous with dread.

As Emily's anxiety grew, she developed a fear of being alone – especially at night. One night, when a strong breeze animated the tree in a particularly alarming way, she turned up in her mother's room and asked if she could sleep with her.

"No," Emily's mother replied, her voice groggy with Valium-induced sleep. "You're far too old for that."

Emily returned to her own room and cried the night away. At about midday the sound of the phone ringing woke her up. She went downstairs and peered into the kitchen, where she could see her mother speaking on the telephone, her face disconcertingly lively – not at all like the tired, resigned face that Emily had grown accustomed to. Emily asked her mother who had called. "No one," her mother replied, looking embarrassed and quickly changing the subject. That day Emily didn't go out to look for Bagpuss, but followed her mother around the house, even offering to accompany her to the grocery store.

For the next few days, Emily went everywhere with her mother, and now sat watching tensely as her mother relaxed reading a Mills and Boon novel after finishing the housework. Eventually Emily's mother could stand her intent gaze no longer.

"Shouldn't you be out looking for Bagpuss?" she asked.

"He's not coming back," replied Emily morosely. "They never do."

"What's that supposed to mean?"

"Nothing." Emily dropped her gaze to the floor.

"Well, why don't you call those nice girls we met at the grocery store the other day – I'm sure they'd love to play with you."

"I'd rather stay here with you."

"Well, you're going to need to find something to occupy yourself with by the weekend. I'm going out on Saturday."

"What?" Emily looked like she'd been slapped in the face.

"I'm going out on Saturday ... don't look so shocked. I have a right to a life, you know."

"Where are you going?"

"To a dance."

"Who with?"

"Les."

"Who's Les?" Emily was looking increasingly frightened.

"Les... The man who drove us here."

"The cab driver?"

"He drives a cab to earn a living, but he's really a writer."

Emily was trying hard to get a handle on what was happening. After a long pause, she asked, "Can I come?"

"No, Emily. You can't come."

"Fine," said Emily, and ran out of the room so that her mother wouldn't see the tears welling up in her eyes. Her mother was going to leave her. With the cab driver. First her father, then Bagpuss, and now her mother. Emily would die here – in this big dark house – get sick and die all alone, and by the time they found her body it would be mauled by rats and covered in spiders, and flies would have laid their eggs in her and she would be crawling with maggots. She had to stop her mother leaving.

Emily put her coat on and headed out of the house.

"Where are you going?" Her mother came out of the sitting room.

"I'm going to play with the kids we met at the grocery store."

"Oh." The sudden U-turn surprised Emily's mother. Then again, Emily was almost a teenager now, and her strange, unpredictable behaviour was probably just a symptom of her age.

It was getting late by the time Emily returned from the internet cafe, hiding a bunch of printouts behind her back as her mother questioned her about what she had been doing with the girls from the grocery store. Emily seemed calmer at dinner than she had been for a while, and her mother was pleased that her new friends were helping her to get over Bagpuss's disappearance.

But Emily was more anxious than ever, and that night she had the nightmare again. She was stumbling after Bagpuss through the meadow at the back of her house, the sky lit up by dry lightning, and the flowers and weeds mutating painfully into grotesque animals and birds that pecked and snapped at her heels, screeching wildly. The sky grew darker and, as Emily reached the river, she heard a splash and threw herself into the inky water, crying out her pet's name. But as Emily reached the spot where her cat had gone under the water for the last time, as she dived down and grabbed him, it was not Bagpuss she pulled out of the murky depths, it was the pale-faced corpse of her mother. Emily screamed and woke herself up. She got out of bed and crept to her mother's room, standing silently for long minutes and listening to her mother's regular breathing as she slept.

Emily was determined to go through with her plan. And she had to act fast as Saturday was only two days away. The poison was easy enough to buy, as many of the rural houses had problems with rats, and the local store stocked a variety of rodent-killing products. Emily's research provided her with all the information she needed to carry out her plan. The idea had first come to her when she remembered a murder mystery she had seen on television: a man had killed his wife over the period of a year by giving her small amounts of poison in her food – too small to kill her immediately, but enough to make his wife progressively more sick until eventually she died. Of course Emily did not want to kill her mother – quite the opposite. She wanted her mother to stay with her forever. She would never give her mother enough poison to make her really sick; just enough to make her feel a little poorly. Emily would look after her mother and tend to her every need, so that after a while her mother would not even want to go out; she would come to rely on Emily, to appreciate her and be grateful for her company. And she certainly would not want to leave with the cab driver.

That evening Emily's mother was in a strange mood. It would have been her fourteenth wedding anniversary if her husband hadn't left her. She couldn't for the life of her remember if she had taken her Valium or not. Emily was being neurotic again, following her around the house and trying to talk to her, but she was far too tired to cope with Emily's quirks today. When Emily surprised her by making her a cup of hot chocolate, she took the mug, but decided to drink it in bed.

Emily's mother placed the mug on her bedside table and went to the bathroom cabinet. Perhaps she hadn't taken her Valium after all. She took one out of the prescription bottle and, after a moment's hesitation, she took out another. She carried the pills through to her bedroom and, climbing into bed, washed them down with the hot chocolate. After a while she started to feel sick. She doubled up in pain and reached out for the bedside table to steady herself, knocking off the lamp, which smashed on the floor.

Emily heard the noise in her mother's room and rushed over. The sight that greeted her was more terrifying than any nightmare she had ever had. Her mother was thrashing around in the bed, blood and vomit all over her nightgown.

"Mummy!"

By the time the ambulance arrived, the suffering of Emily's mother was over. After pronouncing the woman dead, the paramedic looked around the house for the girl who had called in to say that her mother was very sick.

Emily headed across the wilderness, her movements slowed by the stones and pebbles that were stretching the pockets of her coat. She barely noticed the nettles that stung her ankles and the thistles that scratched her arms. Her eyes were fixed on the tree line beyond the river and she thought she could see the tip of Bagpuss's tail ahead of her in the darkness. As she reached the riverbank, there was a splash, and the inky water closed over her head as she fell forward and allowed the stones and the current to pull her down.

WHERE THE STORIES WERE PREVIOUSLY PUBLISHED:

SCHRÖDINGER'S HUMAN – *The Fifth Black Book of Horror* (2009) ed. Charles Black, pub. Mortbury Press.

LITTLE PIG – *The Eighth Black Book of Horror* (2011) ed. Charles Black, pub. Mortbury Press; *Best Horror of the Year Volume Four* (2012) ed. Ellen Datlow, pub. Night Shade Books.

BUY A GOAT FOR CHRISTMAS – *Best New Werewolf Tales* (2012) ed. Carolina Smart, pub. Books of the Dead Press.

CUT! – *The Screaming Book of Horror* (2012) ed. Johnny Mains, pub. Screaming Dreams.

ARTHUR'S CELLAR – *No Monsters Allowed* (2013) ed. Alex Davis, publ. Dog Horn Publishing.

THE APPRENTICE – *The Ninth Black Book of Horror* (2012) ed. Charles Black, pub. Mortbury Press.

THE GIRL IN THE BLUE COAT – *Exotic Gothic 5 [Volume 1]* (2013) ed. Danel Olson, pub. PS Publishing.

RUSALKA – *Postscripts #28/29 Exotic Gothic 4* (2012) ed. Danel Olson, pub. PS Publishing.

FIRST NIGHT – *Dark World* (2013) ed. Timothy Parker Russell, pub. Tartarus Press.

HALLOWEEN LIGHTS – *And Now The Nightmare Begins: The Horror Zine* (2009) ed. Jeani Rector, pub. BearManor Media; *Halloween Dances with the Dead* (2010), ed. Jean Goldstrom, pub. Whortleberry Press.

THE COFFIN – *His Red Eyes Again* (2013) ed. Julia Kruk and Tracy Lee, pub. The Dracula Society.

THE CREAKING – *The Seventh Black Book of Horror* (2010) ed. Charles Black, pub. Mortbury Press.

UNDERBELLY – *The Unspoken* (2013) ed. William Meikle, pub. Karōshi Books.

TEA WITH THE DEVIL – *Strange Halloween* (2012), ed. Jean Goldstrom, pub. Whortleberry Press.

ELEGY – *This Hermetic Legislature: A Homage to Bruno Schulz* (2012) ed. D.P. Watt and D.T. Ghetu, pub. Ex Occidente Press, (published under the title ETUDE).

BAGPUSS – *The Sixth Black Book of Horror* (2010) ed. Charles Black, pub. Mortbury Press (short version); *Best New Writing 2011* (2010), exec. ed. Christopher Klim, pub. Hopewell Publications LLC (full version).

FISH and DIRTY DYBBUK original to this collection.

Lightning Source UK Ltd.
Milton Keynes UK
UKOW04f0822300415

250634UK00001B/20/P